CRITICS RAVE FOR
STEVEN TORRES AND
PRECINCT PUERTO RICO!

"A most promising start to a new procedural series."
—*Library Journal* (Starred Review)

"A fine debut that will leave readers clamoring for an encore."
Booklist

"A top-notch police procedural whose engrossing details create an authentic feel. Terse, deadpan prose, believable characters, and an offbeat setting add up to a promising series kickoff."
—*Kirkus Reviews* (Starred Review)

"Steven Torres has crafted a fascinating tale about illegal immigration and the clash between good and corrupt cops in Puerto Rico."
—José Latour, Author of *Outcast*

"Steven Torres knows what he's doing. He has captured life on the edge of Puerto Rican society with a creepy realism that is consistently well-drawn, powerful, political, and which builds at a furious pace."
—K.j.a. Wishnia, Edgar-nominated Author of *Red House*

PERSONAL JUSTICE

"That guy started it," Marcos mumbled.

The deputy felt a strong urge to get Marcos to say more, but he checked himself. If he started Marcos talking without a lawyer, with his lawyer sitting only a hundred yards away, he might jeopardize the case. Better to leave Marcos to mumble to himself without a reply.

With his free hand, Vargas opened the station house door, and they both stepped out into the sunlight. The sun was beginning its slow summer descent and shone directly in the officer's eyes. He squinted, and when he looked up Gonzalo was waving him on from the corner twenty yards away. Vargas gave his prisoner a slight push toward the sheriff, but Marcos refused to move.

"He started it," he said out loud.

"I heard you the first time," Vargas said.

He pushed a little harder and Marcos had no choice but to move forward.

"He started it," he repeated. This time he was speaking loudly to someone else, and he was crying.

"I'm not doing anything to you…," Vargas said.

"It wasn't me, it wasn't me! Don't kill me!" Marcos screamed, and he tried to break free from the officer.

Vargas looked up to see his sheriff running toward him, but it was too late. Closer still, coming out from between two cars was Perfecto Cruz. At his side, in his right hand, he held an ax.

Other *Leisure* books by Steven Torres:

PRECINCT PUERTO RICO

DEATH
IN PRECINCT
PUERTO RICO

STEVEN TORRES

LEISURE BOOKS NEW YORK CITY

A LEISURE BOOK®

March 2007

Published by

Dorchester Publishing Co., Inc.
200 Madison Avenue
New York, NY 10016

Copyright © 2003 by Steven Torres
Previously published by St. Martin's Press

ISBN 0-8439-5831-6

The name "Leisure Books" and the stylized "L" with design are trademarks of Dorchester Publishing Co., Inc.

Printed in the United States of America.

Visit us on the web at www.dorchesterpub.com.

*This book is dedicated to
Luz Maria and Jose Luis,
who both helped make me the man I am,
and to Damaris,
who loves me even though.*

DEATH
IN PRECINCT
PUERTO RICO

CHAPTER ONE

After giving birth to a healthy, nine-pound boy, and spending a night of rest in the city hospital in Comerio, Elena Maldonado called Luis Gonzalo, the sheriff of Angustias. She would need a ride home, she explained to him, and Gonzalo told her over the phone that she did not need to say anymore. He would be there when she was discharged that afternoon.

"What are you going to do?" his wife Mari asked when he had finished reassuring Elena about how little trouble the whole thing would be and finally put down the phone.

"What do you mean, 'What are you going to do?' I'm going to take her home. What else should I do?"

"Can't you bring her here?" Mari asked.

"Where?"

"Here."

1

"Here? How am I going to bring her here? She has a home, a husband . . ."

"He's a monster," Mari said emphatically. In her mind, a monster had nothing like the rights that a true husband should expect.

"True, we don't have to like him. . . ."

"He beats her."

"She married him. She remains married. . . ."

"He. Beats. Her," Mari repeated as though explaining something to a child.

"She should get a divorce."

"She should kill him," Mari answered.

"I don't see—"

"Stab him in his sleep."

It was clear that Mari had given the idea more than casual thought.

"Okay, Mari. You win. Still, I have to take her to her house. If she wants to file for divorce, I'll take her straight to Maria Garcia. I'll even pay the fee to file the forms, okay?"

Mari muttered something and gave her husband a stare that would have caused him to check himself for bleeding had he not been an expert in her various moods.

He dressed into his civilian clothes, got into his car and drove off to the Angustias station house just off the town's plaza.

Like other towns in Puerto Rico, Angustias had been built around a central plaza, complete with fountain, trees, and benches. Unlike many of the larger towns (and which towns were not larger than Angustias?) the plaza had maintained its importance through the centuries. The Roman Catholic church still stood on one side, and the *alcaldia* still faced it across the plaza. Both buildings were still used for their original purposes. The townspeople still congregated on the plaza for saints' festivals, *fiestas patronales*, and they ate their lunch there.

Inside the station house, Gonzalo's senior deputy Hector Pareda was taking lunch with his partner. Gonzalo was experimenting with a new schedule so that it was Gonzalo and his partner, Wilfrido Vargas, who were supposed to relieve Hector and Anibal Gomez at two in the afternoon.

"Hey chief!" Gomez yelled out, as Gonzalo entered the station house. He had adopted the annoying habit of referring to Gonzalo as anything but Gonzalo or sheriff.

Gonzalo smiled wanly. There was no breaking people out of this habit once they had become infected. Hector certainly had proven incurable.

"I'm going over to pick up Elena Maldonado. She gave birth yesterday. Wilfrido will relieve you guys, but he might need a little help. Anyway, I might be back in time . . ."

"When's her checkout time?" Hector asked.

"At one."

"That's plenty of time."

The way Hector drove an hour might be enough to cross the entire island.

3

"Well, there are always delays . . ."

"Just flash your badge, chief!" Gomez yelled again. Though Gonzalo was only a yard away from him, Gomez was a bit hyperactive and had a tendency to speak louder than strictly necessary.

"Yeah, well, just give Wilfrido whatever help he needs if I don't get back in time."

The deputies agreed, and the sheriff left the station house. It was a little after noon when Gonzalo climbed back into his car and started out for the hospital in Comerio.

The road from Angustias to Comerio is downhill and filled with tight curves so that it somewhat resembles a skier's slalom course or perhaps a snake slithering its way among bushes and tree trunks. Especially high in the hills, there is a dense canopy of vines and branches covering parts of the road so that daylight sometimes looks like twilight and twilight like the night. The effect of the sun and blue sky peeping through the dark green of this canopy can be mesmerizing, and Gonzalo remembered that he had been called to this road several times because nonnatives driving through had paid more attention to their peekaboo game with the sky than to the road ahead of them.

At the hospital in Comerio, Gonzalo approached the front desk, explained his cause and was lead to Elena's room on the first floor by an orderly with a large grin.

"I'm not the father," Gonzalo told the young man.

The young man nodded and raised an eyebrow ever so slightly, seeming to suggest that he knew better.

The orderly swung the door open.

"There's your baby," he announced.

"I'm not the father." Gonzalo tried again, but the orderly merely tilted his head back a fraction and broadened his grin as if to reassure the sheriff that the secret was safe.

In the room, the mother was nursing her child. Gonzalo reminded himself that he had seen the same scene a dozen times before and that it was a completely natural act. He still would rather have been elsewhere at that moment.

"Do you want me to come back?" he asked looking at the floor.

"Why?" Elena asked.

Gonzalo could think of no good reply. Instead, he nodded and bowed his way out of the room as though complying with some unsaid order. He stood in the hall, watching the clock strike out five minutes.

Elena Maldonado was young but carried a tired look with her everywhere. Her struggle with life had been great in her twenty or so years, and it had taken its toll on her thin frame and face. Her body bore scars of fights with her husband and before that her father. It was said that she had the spirit to fight back for a while but never enough body to hurt the men who attacked her. Her punches had always only been enough to enrage them further. Gonzalo had never seen her fight her attackers. He had twice found her in a heap in a corner of her cement home and had once found her pinned under the weight of her husband, covering her face with her arms while he pummeled her. He had never seen her fight back. Nor had he ever seen a mark on the men who had beaten her.

Still, even Doña Carmen, a woman whose word he had respected all his life, insisted that Elena was capable of putting up a fight. Standing in the hallway of the Comerio hospital, Gonzalo thought of this claim. Having just seen her looking so tired and drawn, it seemed impossible that she could ever present a threat to any man. Even to his deputy Gomez who was nothing more than five feet tall and probably only a dozen pounds over a hundred in weight.

When he reentered the room, Elena was standing, putting the baby back into its bassinet.

"Can I help you with that?" Gonzalo asked, but there was nothing to help with.

"Maybe you can carry my bag?" Elena offered.

"Sure."

Gonzalo was nervous without any real reason, and he was anxious to have something to do. He led her through the paperwork and out the door of the hospital. He made sure the baby's car seat was properly strapped in on the backseat, reassuring Elena that her child would be fine without her during the

6

ride though she hadn't said anything about being separated from the child.

Gonzalo drove back to Angustias slowly. He wanted the time to think of what to say to his young passenger. He really did want to advise her to divorce her husband, but as an officer of the law, it wasn't his place to do so. In any event, he knew Elena as a young woman who had not finished high school and never held a job. Her husband worked only erratically, but he did usually pay the bills. With a child, it would be doubly difficult for her to leave the man who beat her. The sheriff did not know how to approach the topic, and he did not know whether the topic should be approached at all.

"I need to go to Maria Garcia's house for a few minutes before you take me home," Elena whispered, staring straight ahead.

Maria Garcia was one of three lawyers living in Angustias. The other two were old and had given up trying to compete with Ms. Garcia. Garcia handled contract law and most of the real estate transactions in Angustias now passed through her hands. She also handled divorces.

Gonzalo wanted to ask about this stop at the lawyer's house, but he decided to keep quiet and focus on the road.

Maria Garcia had moved to Angustias after getting a law degree from a New York university. She was young and beautiful and worked very hard with a professional manner that her clients appreciated but which baffled her rival lawyers. To them, lawsuits just normally took years and hundreds of billable hours, and they could see no reason to inform clients of the boring details of a suit that could decide whether they were rich or bankrupt. To them, there was no point in explaining the contracts they had their clients sign. Maria Garcia worked differently, making sure the client was informed of every step and understood each step as it was taken. This won her accounts that the other two lawyers had long split between themselves.

At the time of Elena's visit, Ms. Garcia was in her mid-thirties. Her Nuyorican accent was still noticeable, but then she spoke so quickly, it would have been hard to understand her no matter what accent she had. Her house was one of those built more than a century before along the perimeter of the town's plaza. There were only a few larger or more prestigious in Angustias, and no one doubted Ms. Garcia had the means to have done better.

Gonzalo parked outside and shut off the car. Elena climbed out of the car and walked as quickly as she could toward Garcia's front door. She gave the sheriff no guarantee that she would only be few minutes, nor did she take her newborn. Gonzalo was left to pray that the mother made it back before the baby awoke from its sleeping peace.

A few minutes later, Elena was walking out of the lawyer's house. Maria Garcia stood at the door; she made eye contact with the sheriff in his car, but was poker-faced. As Elena settled back into the passenger seat, she folded a stapled set of papers into quarters and stuffed it into her baby bag. Gonzalo started up his car and drove on, headed to Elena's house.

After a few minutes of silence and as they neared her driveway, the sheriff spoke.

"Are you in any trouble?" he asked. He spoke slowly, not wanting to startle either of his passengers, and he gave only the slightest glance in Elena's direction.

She looked straight ahead and said nothing, leaving Gonzalo to fill the silence that grew unbearable to him.

"I might be able to help . . . I mean, maybe there is something I can . . . I mean, I know a lot of people, and if you're having . . ."

"I'm getting a divorce," Elena said. Apparently the noise of Gonzalo's fumblings had grown unbearable to her.

"I've had enough of Marcos." She continued: "He's not a good man. You know what he does. I'm not going to raise a child that sees me afraid everyday, that sees me beaten every week."

The sheriff pulled into the driveway and turned off the car engine. Before unbuckling his seat belt, he made a quick survey of the Maldonado home. It was a one-floor cinder-block home with a roof of corrugated zinc. Most of the outside had been painted pink; the rest had been neglected altogether. The nearest neighbor was at least a hundred yards further down the road, around a slight bend. The house sat at the head of the acres Marcos owned and occasionally worked. At the moment, it had a forlorn look of abandonment, almost as though it were struggling to be a farm but the untamed nature around it was too much. Weeds and vines encroached.

"Something wrong?" Elena asked.

"No." Gonzalo unbuckled his seat belt but made no move to open his door.

"I was just wondering if it was you who decided to paint the house pink. Pink doesn't match my vision of Marcos."

"Marcos picked it."

"Maybe he thought he was pleasing you?" Gonzalo tried. Now that the marriage was nearing its end, he felt a need to salvage at least one happy moment from what he knew to be an unmitigated disaster of a union.

"Maybe he thought that," Elena replied. "Marcos never asked me what I wanted. He usually just wants the cheapest. Marcos wants to please Marcos."

With that, Elena got out of the car, and Gonzalo followed suit. Together they retrieved the baby from the backseat. Elena took hold of the car seat, but Gonzalo didn't release it.

"Have you told Marcos of your plans?"

"Is it your business?" Elena asked. This was the first clear sign of defiance Gonzalo had ever noticed in her.

"Given his past behavior, there is a good chance he'll react violently whenever you tell him. That makes it my business. Have you told him?"

"No. When the paperwork's done, I'll tell him and walk out the door to my parents' house."

Gonzalo still wouldn't let go of the car seat.

"Promise me one thing. Don't tell him when you're alone with him. Make sure there are plenty of people nearby. Big people. Tell him in the plaza or in the church."

"Don't worry about me. Marcos can't do anything worse to me than he's already done. I'm too tough for him. That makes him even angrier. He can't kill me."

"Don't be foolish, Elena. The difference between him beating you and him killing you is you hitting your head on a rock when you fall."

"Then I won't tell him when I'm near any rocks," she answered.

Gonzalo let go of the car seat and escorted Elena to the door of Maldonado home. The door was already unlocked, and Elena pushed it in.

Marcos was sprawled on the sofa that dominated the front room. He was sound asleep. Gonzalo quickly counted seven empty cans of beer and one half-finished pint of Bacardi. He gave Marcos a shake, but Marcos's brain had been switched off by alcohol, and it wouldn't be coming on again any time soon.

Gonzalo looked to the new mother, and she shrugged.

"Celebrating," she said.

Elena had the baby out of its car seat, and it was awake in her arms, its eyes squinted shut, its entire face marked with a confused frown. It seemed to be trying to decide whether crying was the appropriate response to being awake. Gonzalo knew it was a matter of time, no more than seconds, before the child realized it had no other options.

"Here's my card," he said, pulling one from his wallet.

"Just put it on the table," Elena said as the baby started to cry and she started to pull up her shirt, oblivious to Gonzalo's squeamishness.

Gonzalo did as he was told and went to the door. He stopped and asked without turning,

"What's the child's name?"

"I haven't decided yet," Elena said.

The baby quieted quickly, and Gonzalo knew it had found what it was looking for. He left the house and sat in his car a minute or two savoring the stillness coming from the Maldonado home. Then he went home to change into his uniform and drove to work.

CHAPTER TWO

Mari bombarded her husband with questions as soon as he came in, but he was in a rush to get to work, and he had almost no useful information. He didn't know the size and weight of the child, and there was not yet a name. He could tell her it was a boy, but there was little to say about the father's reaction. He decided not to mention the planned divorce as he knew it would keep him away from his work.

"I've got to get to work, Mari. We'll talk all about it when I get a chance to call you from the station house." He gave Mari a hurried kiss and left for work before she could get a hold of him.

By the time Gonzalo got to the precinct, it was 2:30, and the building was empty. There was no note on the desk, no message on the bulletin board, so the sheriff of Angustias was left to wonder what emergency had called his deputies away. He decided to wander out to the plaza. It being Saturday, there

13

were no schoolchildren to shepherd home and there were only a few people occupying the benches.

"Did they catch him?" Justino Marquez asked. Justino was near to a hundred years of age and had taken the same seat in the plaza each weekend for decades.

"Catch who?" Gonzalo asked, hoping for useful information about his officers' whereabouts.

"Well, you're the sheriff. You tell me."

"Don Justino. Did my deputies tell you where they were going?"

"They didn't say anything to me," Don Justino said. He turned his face away from Gonzalo as if to prove his disinterest in the entire matter.

"Did you overhear anything? Please. It could be very important." This was a game Gonzalo didn't appreciate, but he knew that Don Justino had long ago reached an age when day-to-day activities might begin to seem petty.

"Colmado Ruiz," the old man said, still not bothering to face the sheriff.

"Thank you, Don Justino. I will make sure you receive a commendation from the city." Gonzalo tossed this last over his shoulder as he was walking back towards the precinct. Don Justino still did not look at the sheriff, but his lips pursed into a faint smile at the thought of the official recognition about to be showered on him.

Colmado Ruiz was one of the few places to buy anything in Angustias without having to be near the center of town. With a disappointing selection of canned goods on the shelf and a refrigerator, two pool tables with shabby green felt, and a dozen bottles of island rum and American whiskey and a stack of Dixie cups behind the checkout counter, Colmado Ruiz served as grocery store, pool hall, and bar. The condition of the building mirrored that of its longtime owner: short, wide, and disheveled. Colmado Ruiz was then painted a brilliant yellow with a mud-dark brown for trim. Rafael Ruiz was wearing his habitual dull yellow guayabera and a pair of black polyester slacks. On his feet, a pair of white dress socks and black leather slippers. He stood out in the parking area in front of his store as Gonzalo drove up and waved him in with the stump of his left arm, the hand having been lost some years earlier in a holdup.

"He's crazy!" the squat man shouted as Gonzalo put his car in park.

"He's crazy!"

"Who's crazy?" the sheriff asked. The squad car was parked in front of the store.

"Marrero. He's in there. He . . . He . . . Go take a look. You're the sheriff. Do something with him."

Marrero had been born to make trouble and had plied his trade faithfully for all his almost forty years. He was tall and painfully thin and wore his dark hair at shoulder length. He could have been handsome in a way, but alcohol and fighting had stolen any chance of that. As it was, when Gonzalo walked into the store, Eduardo Marrero was standing on one of the pool tables, his shirt open, the bones of his chest countable, there was a several days' growth of beard stubble, and his hair was stringy with neglect and sweat. In one hand he had the thickest three feet of a pool cue, the end having been snapped off. The other hand held a rum bottle.

In a corner, behind Marrero, Gonzalo could see Deputy Iris Calderon with her arm around a girl of twelve or so. It looked as though she had been a victim of Marrero's pool cue. She was shaking and crying and holding a handkerchief to the side of her head.

As a father of three girls, nothing made Gonzalo angrier than the thought of a young girl abused. He thought it the lowest thing a man could do, and he was in no mood to negotiate Marrero off the pool table.

Officers Gomez and Pareda were positioned at corner pockets facing Marrero. Officer Guillermo Estrada, Calderon's partner, stood directly in front of the drunken man. All three officers had their nightsticks drawn. Marrero kept them at bay by swinging the pool cue, alternating between windmill and Zorro fashion, sometimes lunging at one or the other, sometimes waving the stick lazily as he took a swig from his bottle. His erratic behavior kept the officers from making a coordinated move against the man, and, as Gonzalo found out later, both Pareda and Estrada had rationalized that since the damage to the girl had already been done, the best policy would be to wait until Marrero tired and gave up. But if Gonzalo was in no mood for negotiation, he was certainly in no mood for inaction.

He grabbed a loose pool cue and tapped Estrada's shoulder, signaling him to move to one side. Then he swung at Marrero's legs and was amazed to see Marrero skip over the cue while his lips were still stuck to the bottle. Gonzalo swung again, but Marrero parried the blow as Errol Flynn might have.

While laughing at the sheriff's discomfiture, however, Marrero failed to notice Hector Pareda walking around behind him. Hector grabbed him by the ankles and gave him a sharp pull, toppling him forward towards Gonzalo and Estrada. The sheriff stepped back out of the path of Marrero's fall and let the drunken man hit the ceramic tiles of the store. As Marrero tried to get to his knees, Gonzalo gave him a kick and put a foot between his shoulder blades, pinning him to the floor.

Gonzalo glanced at the corner where his deputy and the girl were both watching the commotion with interest. The girl wiped away a tear and made eye contact with the sheriff, and he pressed down harder on the criminal.

"Hey! What are you trying to do? Kill me?" Marrero yelled from the floor.

Gonzalo looked back to his prisoner.

"Would anyone care if I did?" he asked.

"Did what?" Marrero wanted to know.

"Killed you."

"I would!" Marrero answered. He wasn't as drunk as he seemed.

"Get him out of here," Gonzalo said.

Hector and Officer Estrada each grabbed an arm and wrestled Marrero to his feet. Gonzalo turned his attention to Calderon and the girl. The twelve-year-old was Anna Cardenas. Her father owned a small farm about a quarter of a mile up the road from the store. Gonzalo knew they lived with two other of her siblings and that Tomas Cardenas was a single parent, but at the moment he couldn't bring to mind who the girl's siblings were and why her mother did not live with them.

Anna had clear blue eyes and dark brown hair, but the eyes had tears in them and the hair was partially matted by her own blood. Gonzalo made a quick assessment of the girl's situation. She had apparently been hit once with the pool cue. The blow had raised a welt near her right eye. The welt was bright red and swelling, so that the skin was taut and shiny. The line of raised flesh continued on past her hairline where it became an open cut. Gonzalo estimated it would need six or seven stitches to close the gash.

"You're going to be all right, Anna. You're going

to be all right. Officer Calderon is going to drive you to the clinic. I'm going to talk to your father. Marrero is going to jail. I don't think you'll see him again until you're in high school; maybe not until you're married already.

"Take her to the clinic and get her stitched up. I'll follow a little later with her father," he told his deputy.

Calderon nodded and helped the girl across the store towards the exit.

"Where's Vargas?" Gonzalo asked her.

"He's already at the clinic. . . ."

"He got hurt?"

"Nah, just a few whacks across his back. He didn't even feel them. Marrero just whacked this other guy across the face, busted open his nose. That's how this whole thing got started. Vargas drove him over to be checked out and for a few stitches."

Calderon went out with the girl, put her into her own car and drove off. Though the precinct's budget had been increased and there were now two squad cars, only Hector and Guillermo Estrada liked using them. The other four officers preferred using their own cars. He couldn't vouch for the others, but Gonzalo thought the blue-and-white patrol too formal. He felt like an invader in the squad car, and he preferred to feel like a neighbor.

Rafael Ruiz entered the store as Officer Calderon left, and Gonzalo went up to him.

"What happened here?" he asked the store owner.

"How am I supposed to know?" Ruiz said shrugging his shoulders and moving behind the counter. "That guy is crazy. I won't serve him again. Not until he pays for the bottles he broke."

Ruiz pointed to the floor behind the counter. There were four or five broken bottles and a puddle of alcohol. He crouched with the stump of his left hand on the counter to keep his balance and started to pick up the larger pieces of glass and toss them into a small wastebasket.

"Could you tell me what happened before you pick up the bottles?"

"I told you, I don't know. This guy came in asking for directions. He wanted to know where the *carro publico* stand was, I was telling him. I told him, 'It's a long walk . . . It's better to try to get a ride with one of the customers or go out into the street and ask for *pon* from whoever passes by.' He didn't want to listen to me. I was explaining how to get to the *carro publico* stand. Marrero came in, drunk. He started picking a fight with the guy."

"Did he know the guy? Was this a fight they had started somewhere else?" Gonzalo asked.

"How am I supposed to know? No. I don't think so. He never used the guy's name. He just came in and started calling him names. Then he gave him a push, the guy pushed back, Marrero tripped him, gave him a kick in the gut. That's when I called the precinct. If I had both hands, I'd take care of the trouble myself, but it's hard to pull guys apart when you only have one hand. . . ."

Rafael Ruiz was by no means overly sensitive, but when he spoke of his missing hand, he could not keep from getting lost in memory. At this moment, he looked intently at his stump. He had lost the hand only a few years earlier to robbers on a rainy night when Gonzalo had arrived one minute too late to prevent the tragedy. Remembering the night brought no comfort to the sheriff though he had defeated three men in a drawn-out gunfight. He had been commended by the governor, and the attention of the island had been focused on Angustias for a few days, but to Gonzalo the missing hand symbolized nothing more than that he had failed to get to the scene in time to save a good man from lifelong horror.

"I'm not blaming you for anything, Ruiz. You did the right thing. One question. How did the girl get hurt? How was she involved?"

"That was an accident, I think. Marrero broke the pool cue, hit the guy in the face. The guy fell down to his knees. As he was falling, Marrero took another swing. This time he missed. The girl was walking in and she caught the end of the swing. Goddamn Marrero. I hope you lock him up for a year."

"It should be more than that."

Gonzalo went out to his car and sat in it a moment trying to think of a good way to tell Mr. Cardenas about what had happened to his little girl. Nothing came to mind, and he decided to get it over with as quickly as possible.

As he drove up to the wooden shack the Cardenas family called home, Gonzalo remembered how it was the family came to be motherless. Sonia Cardenas had simply left one day, leaving a note behind that said *Me voy*—"I'm going." After a decade of poverty, there apparently was not much to be said, and Tomas Cardenas had hardly complained after the first few days of disorientation. For a week after she had gone, he lived with some hope that she would return. After that, the hope flickered out, and Tomas became pathetic. Working on his farm became his life with only occasional stops in town for groceries and supplies. He attended parent-teacher conferences in the ridiculous attire of the suit he had been married in, his only suit, leaving off only the bow tie he probably couldn't knot.

Gonzalo knocked on the door and after a minute it was opened by a girl still dressed in pajamas who appeared to be no more than seven.

"Where's your father?" Gonzalo started brusquely since he couldn't remember the girl's name.

She pointed to the back of the shack without saying a word and moved out of the way, so Gonzalo walked into the house, announcing himself with a loud "hello?" No one answered him and he continued on through the house to the back door, which was open wide to the farm out back.

Outside, Tomas was about fifty yards away from

the house trying to remove a tree stump. His horse was tied to the stump with one rope, another rope was slung over his own shoulder and both beasts of burden were straining to disinter a knot of roots that had clearly been in place for decades. Gonzalo picked up an ax from the ground near the roots and started hacking down at one particularly thick trunk. In five minutes, he worked up a sweat that ran down his back and stopped at his waistband. In another five minutes, the root ball tore free from the earth.

Gonzalo spoke as Tomas undid the ropes.

"I've got some bad news for you, Tomas."

Tomas said nothing and coiled the rope for storage.

"Your daughter was hurt in Colmado Ruiz. Not too bad. She'll need a few stitches."

Tomas looked up to the sky and then down to the ground, and Gonzalo imagined that he was trying to connect this news with the disappearance of his wife somehow.

"She at the clinic?" he asked finally.

"Yup."

"She going to stay overnight?"

"I don't think that's going to be necessary. . . ."

"How much is this going to cost?" Tomas asked without looking up.

"If you don't have money, the clinic treats people for free. . . ."

"I didn't say I don't have. I just need to know how much."

23

"You can ask at the clinic. Do you want a ride?"

"I'll go in my truck. I need to get washed up a little."

Gonzalo nodded, not wanting to vocally confirm a statement so undeniably true.

"I'll see you over there in twenty or thirty minutes, okay? I just need to get to the station house for a minute," Gonzalo said, then he turned to go.

"Thanks," Tomas said to the sheriff's back.

"I don't like to bring bad news—" Gonzalo started.

"For the help with the roots. You didn't have to. Thank you."

"A little sweat is good for the soul," Gonzalo said, and Tomas, who was drenched in sweat most of the days of his life, seemed not to understand.

In the precinct, Gonzalo found Hector sitting at a desk engrossed in reading the sports section of a newspaper. Marrero was sleeping on his stomach on a cot in one of the holding cells at the back. His hands were cuffed behind him.

"You can let him out of the cuffs," Gonzalo said.

"We tried that. Estrada's at the clinic getting his face stitched up," Hector answered.

"What are you talking about?"

"He seemed calm. We let him out of his cuffs to fingerprint him, and he tried to escape. He gave Estrada a pretty good push into the bars, and he took a swing at me."

"Then what?"

"Then Anibal brought him down with a club to the back of his head, boss."

"Really?"

"It was a home run," Hector confirmed.

"Maybe we should have the doctor take a look at him."

"You're the sheriff, but if you're asking my opinion, I think the bump on his head is the least of his troubles. Three assaults, one of them on a police officer, attempted escape. It's not going to look good on his résumé."

"How's Estrada?"

"He'll live. He's got a small cut over his right eye. We couldn't get it to stop bleeding, and he said he was feeling a little dizzy, so I had Anibal drive him to the clinic. I figure he'll miss a shift or two and be as good as new."

"He's not going to like having a cut on his face," Gonzalo noted.

He was alluding to Estrada's streak of vanity. The sheriff had known Estrada for only a brief time, but though the deputy was experienced and capable, Gonzalo thought him a bit too proud of his good looks. He had to remind himself that what Estrada thought of his looks was his own business. One couldn't look down on a man who in every other way was an asset to the town of Angustias.

Gonzalo glanced at his watch.

"I'm sorry, Hector. I'm relieving you later than I thought. We'll add that to your compensatory time. . . ."

"I've got fourteen hours of comp time."

"I know. In another week, when the new people are fully broken in, I'm giving you and Iris a couple of days off. Right now I need to make sure they're all set to take care of Angustias. I don't think they know most of the back roads yet."

"I think I'd rather have the money. . . ."

"I can put in the requisition for it, but it'll be rejected. It'll take ten weeks. . . ."

Hector put up his hand to stop the sheriff. He knew from experience how hard it could be to see a request for more money through to fruition.

He got up and strapped on his gun belt.

"Could you do me a favor?" Gonzalo asked.

"Sure thing, chief."

"I have to go to the clinic. Could you check in on Elena Maldonado on your way home? Just see how she's doing. Say you want a look at the baby. It is a very beautiful baby."

"Are there ugly babies?" Hector asked.

"I've seen a few," Gonzalo answered.

A minute or two later and both men were on the road toward their separate destinations. Marrero was left on the cot in his holding cell to sleep himself back to consciousness.

CHAPTER THREE

La Clinica Mendoza, as the only medical facility in Angustias was called, had started as an underfunded site serving all the poor of the town—essentially the entire population of something over 9,000. Until a few years before there had been only one doctor and one nurse and one examining room. Then the richest man in town (in fact one of the richest on the island) Martin Mendoza had run into some tax difficulty that no one could ever understand. Incomprehensibility aside, Mendoza had decided to pour millions into the clinic rather than face some harsher fate at the hands of tax collectors. There were now three doctors and three nurses and several beds for overnight stays. There were even labs with technicians and an X-ray machine. Perhaps the clearest sign of the new prosperity was that patients now came from neighboring towns for treatment.

In making additions to the clinic itself, the parking lot had been made smaller, but it was hard to notice the difference. There was still more than an acre of parking, and even with the extra traffic, there was space for several dozen more cars. Gonzalo parked close to the clinic and rushed in. He was anxious to settle into some sort of pattern for the day; he wanted to patrol the back roads of Angustias, and he was more than a little upset at the disturbance Marrero had caused.

In the waiting area, there were a total of six people. Two of them were deputies.

"Where's Anibal?" Gonzalo asked.

Only officers Calderon and Vargas were there.

"He took Marrero's first victim to a *carro publico* stand," Officer Calderon answered.

"Did the guy give a statement?" Gonzalo asked.

"Nope. He refused medical treatment. The doctor said there wasn't much he could do for his nose anyway. Then he said it was a fair fight, and he wasn't interested in pressing charges," Vargas said.

"But we're still keeping Marrero. We have to make a case against him because of what he did to the girl. . . ."

Gonzalo paused for emphasis. He wanted to impress upon his partner, a rookie, how important every shred of evidence could be, but he felt this was an uphill battle.

"Next time, if a victim refuses to press charges, let me talk to them before you let them wander away to God knows where."

He paused again, not knowing exactly how long the pause would have to be to get through to Vargas. He sometimes seemed to Gonzalo to be somewhat slow-witted though his college and academy records showed him near the top of his field in every academic subject. Common sense and practical matters seemed to slip through his fingers entirely.

Iris Calderon reached for a *National Geographic* to avoid witnessing Vargas's humiliation. Gonzalo decided to put off scolding his deputy. They would have to have a talk about procedures, but he was beginning to feel a slight headache forming, and he preferred not to aggravate it just then.

"How's Estrada doing?" He changed the subject.

"There's the doctor." Vargas pointed.

At the age of forty-two, Dr. Perez was the oldest of the doctors who worked at the clinic. He had been there more than a decade, and, while he held himself somewhat aloof socially and rarely said anything that wasn't part of a diagnosis or prognosis, he was respected by the *Angustiados*. After all, while other doctors used the clinic merely as a step to some more elevated position, he had decided from the start to stay in Angustias and serve out his career in his adopted hometown.

"How are your patients doing?" Gonzalo asked.

"I have seen seventeen patients this morning. I assume you refer to your deputy?"

"And the girl, Anna Cardenas."

"I expect both to be fine. Each required six

stitches. Deputy Estrada complains of some dizziness. Not unusual for the type of blow he received. I'll have him lie down for an hour or so and see if that clears it up. Both patients are conscious and can speak with you if you want."

"Is the father—" Gonzalo started, but Dr. Perez was already walking away toward an examining room and another patient.

Gonzalo turned to his officers.

"Did Tomas Cardenas show up yet?"

"He went into the room a few minutes and spoke to the girl. I know he told her to wait here in the clinic. Then he just walked out," Officer Calderon answered.

"What do you mean he walked out?"

"Exactly that. He said he'd be back in a little bit to pick up the girl."

"Did he say where he was going?"

"No."

"Did he know about Marrero?"

"Well, yeah. I spoke to him a few minutes. Told him Marrero was in custody. He seemed okay with it."

"Has Tomas ever seemed not okay with anything? Look. I'm going to visit the two patients. Calderon, you go home. Wilfrido, I want you to get back to the precinct and stay there. For all I know, Tomas Cardenas is setting fire to the place right now. Remember this, don't let an angry father out of your sight. That's his little girl in there."

Anna was on an examining room table, half reclined with boredom. She watched listlessly as Gonzalo made his way into the room.

"How are you doing?" Gonzalo tried to sound cheerful.

"I'm okay," she replied without energy.

Gonzalo stroked her hair and revealed a patch of white gauze taped to the scalp over her left ear.

"You won't be able to notice the scar when this heals," Gonzalo predicted.

Anna shrugged, and he thought of her for a moment as a lifeless child who was destined to grow into a lifeless adult for whom no one would particularly care. He purged his mind of the thought as evil.

"Did your father say when he was coming back?"

Anna shrugged again. Gonzalo could see she wanted nothing more than to be allowed to get back into bed and forget the entire day.

"Did he say he where he was going?"

"Home," the girl said.

Gonzalo stroked her hair again lightly and gave her a kiss on the crown of her head. Then he walked out again to the waiting room and told Dr. Perez he would be back in a few minutes. Perez was busy interviewing a patient and gave Gonzalo only a glance of recognition before turning back to his work.

The sheriff left the clinic and drove toward town. He had visions of Tomas Cardenas at that moment peering in at Marrero through the side window of the precinct, maybe squirting him with lighter fluid.

Instead, as he rounded the curve near Colmado
Ruiz, he saw Tomas's pickup parked out in front.
He parked next to it and went into the store. Tomas
was leaning with his elbows on the counter, a Dixie
cup of beer in one hand, in conversation with
Rafael Ruiz. Ruiz had taken a seat on a folding chair
behind the counter.

Gonzalo walked to the refrigerator and pulled
out a Coca-Cola. Condensation formed on the
small glass bottle before he got it to the counter so
that the soda looked as refreshing as it did in the
commercials.

"What are you guys talking about?" Gonzalo
asked, trying to sound unworried.

"Nothing," Ruiz answered. "I was just telling
Tomas how it all happened; how his little girl got
hurt. It was really an accident. Marrero was drunk,
and he was swinging at someone else. He didn't
mean to hit Anna, I'm sure of it."

"But he hit her anyway," Tomas said.

The store was silent for a moment. There was no
disputing his conclusion, but then he had said it in
such a dispassionate voice that he could as easily
have been speaking of yesterday's weather.

"What do you plan to do?" Gonzalo asked.

Tomas ignored the question a moment and took a
sip of his beer.

"The doctor said she might be better off staying
at the clinic for an hour or two. . . . Just to be safe.

Me, I've got two other children at home and work to do. I'll pick her up later in the afternoon." He took another sip of his beer.

"You're not thinking of confronting Marrero, are you?" Gonzalo opened his Coca-Cola and drank down half the bottle waiting for Tomas's reply.

"Is he going to spend some time in jail?" Tomas asked.

"I expect he'll do some time. He assaulted two of my officers. Trust me. He'll be in jail a while."

"Then I have nothing to do with him. Just don't let him cross my path."

Tomas swallowed down the rest of his beer and went out. Gonzalo heard the pickup start up and drive off. He finished his soda and dropped the bottle into a small wastebasket at the end of the counter.

"How much did he have to drink?" he asked.

"Fifty cents," Ruiz said, indicating the price of about a cupful of beer.

"You charged him?" Gonzalo was a bit incredulous. "After what happened here?"

"No, I didn't charge him, it was on the house. He didn't even ask for it, I offered. He just wanted to talk. Anyway, it's not like I hit his daughter. Don't forget, it was Marrero."

"I know, I know. It's just been a bad day already."

He turned to leave, and Ruiz called him back.

"Gonzalo." He called out and the sheriff turned to him.

"Are you planning to pay for that soda?"

Gonzalo paid and stepped out again into the sunlight and heard Hector Pareda's voice coming through loud, clear and anxious over the CB in his car. "I need an ambulance here!" he said. "And I need backup!"

As he would see for himself a few minutes later, while Gonzalo had been speaking to his deputies and Anna Cardenas in the clinic and then Tomas Cardenas in Colmado Ruiz, Hector had found horror at the home of Elena Maldonado.

The front door was ajar when he pulled up to the house. He knocked and announced himself, but no one responded though he saw Marcos's car was parked out front. He pushed the door open and went in.

Inside, Marcos Maldonado was sitting upright on his sofa, his elbows resting on his knees, his head down, a shirt in his hands.

"Everything all right in here, Marcos?" Hector asked, but Marcos didn't move or respond in any way.

Hector took a closer look.

There was a cut on Marcos's right forearm about three inches long, and Hector could see it would need stitching. The shirt in his hands was stained with blood. Hector crouched next to Marcos.

"Do you want me to help you with that?" Hector asked.

He took the shirt from Marcos thinking to use it as a temporary bandage until he could drive Marcos to the clinic. The shirt was actually a woman's blouse. Hector had often seen Elena in it. Now it was torn, and Hector thought it had more blood than the simple cut on Marcos's forearm could have caused.

Marcos looked into Hector's eyes sadly, as though he were seeking an answer.

"How'd this happen Marcos?" Hector asked though he thought he knew.

"I don't know . . . I don't know how this happened." For a moment his eyes seemed to implore Hector for an answer, but when he turned his head away, his eyes lagged behind a bit, and Hector knew he was profoundly drunk. Hector finished knotting the shirt over the wound.

"Where's Elena?" Hector asked.

Marcos turned back to face Hector but seemed not to understand the question.

"Where's Elena?" Hector asked a little louder. He was hoping Elena would answer.

"Where's Elena?" he repeated, but he was sure Marcos wasn't going to give him useful information.

"Where's Elena?" Hector stood up and spoke the words loudly to the rest of the house more than to Marcos.

Marcos looked toward to kitchen.

"Stay here," Hector instructed.

The entire house was tiny, and the walk to the kitchen was a matter of only a few steps. The kitchen was also tiny, so Elena's body and the pool

35

of blood that had drained out of it took up most of the floor space. In fact, with his first step into the room, Hector had nearly stepped onto her hair.

Elena's body was splayed out on the floor, her right foot crooked behind her left calf, her arms up and bent at the elbow so that her hands were level with her head. She had on faded jeans and a white T-shirt. Her feet were bare, her shirt had several bloody puncture holes in it, and her eyes were more wide open than they had ever been in life and staring at the ceiling. She looked as though she were lying on a grassy hill watching clouds go by.

He heard Marcos run out of the front room, but he crouched and felt for Elena's pulse. There was none. He stood again and tried to think for a moment, but nothing would gel in his mind. In his years as an officer he had never stumbled upon a body in this fashion, and it upset him. He heard Marcos running around the back of the house into the woods, and he snapped to action.

Hector was young and a fast runner, but Marcos had a good head start and knew the contours of his property. The Maldonado property was mixed; part of it was nearly flat; when Marcos had the energy, he cleared it of weeds and planted some native vegetables often just to watch them die before harvest. The rest of the land was treacherously inclined and completely overgrown. This was the area Marcos had run into, and Hector knew he was going to have a bad time of following him. He yelled for him to stop, but this had no effect.

The inclined area was thick with trees, dark and cool. It took Hector only a dozen steps or so in this area to lose his footing and slide on the red clay earth. He got up and continued the pursuit a few steps more before slipping again. This second time he traveled a half dozen yards on the seat of his pants before stopping himself with the help of a *guayaba* tree trunk. At this point he decided to give up the pursuit, return to his car, and radio for help.

"I need help here!" He spoke into the CB much louder than he had intended.

It made little difference. No one was on the other end.

"I need an ambulance!" Still no one responded.

He kept begging for assistance for a full minute before Gonzalo's voice answered him.

"What's the matter?"

"I'm at the Maldonado place, chief. She's dead. Marcos is gone. On foot. Into the woods. He just ran off," Hector explained in a hurry.

"Elena's dead?"

"Yup. And Marcos is in the woods somewhere. I need help here. He's headed towards. Martin Mendoza's horse ranch. He could be there in five or six minutes if he keeps going at the rate he was. . . ."

"I'm on my way. Stay with the body. Keep the site secure."

Gonzalo got into his car and pounded his palm into the steering wheel several times, bending it a little. He drove towards the Maldonado home cursing to himself as he went. The day had gotten infinitely worse.

CHAPTER FOUR

Martin Mendoza owned property all over Angustias County and in several over counties scattered throughout Puerto Rico. He sometimes considered himself a farmer though, of course, he had never personally worked a farm and always found it an annoyance that his favorite fruits were inexplicably sometimes out of season. Among his properties was a stable with four or five horses and two dozen acres for them to graze in. He loved horseback riding, but rarely used his own horses because for long stretches he would forget he owned them. Sometimes he didn't remember even when he made a quarterly payment to the bank account of their caretaker.

The land the horses roamed (and they were good horses) sloped gently up and away from the Maldonado property. Somewhere amid the alcohol in his mind, Marcos had the plan of corralling one of these horses and making his escape. The groom watched, disbelieving what he saw. There was no possibility that Marcos would get near one of the horses, and for a moment it seemed as though the horses were playing with the intruder, keeping themselves just out of the reach of the desperate man. After a minute or so the horses decided Marcos was no fun and moved off as a group at a quick trot. Marcos followed them for a few steps but he had already run a great deal. He fell and didn't get up.

The caretaker went into the barn and got out a pistol he hadn't used since the last time a horse broke its leg and went out to the field to see if Marcos wanted to end his trespass. Marcos was still flat on his back, panting when he got out to him.

"What are you doing here?" he asked.

"I'm trying to steal a horse," Marcos answered. "They won't come to me."

"They're not used to you," the caretaker answered.

"I know. Can you give me a hand? Maybe between the two of us . . ."

At this point, Gonzalo called out from near the barn. The groom turned to give the sheriff his attention.

"We're looking for Marcos Maldonado!" Gonzalo yelled. "Have you seen him?"

The groom used his gun to point at Marcos. Gonzalo jogged towards them, and a minute later was at the groom's side, standing over Marcos who was drowsy with exhaustion and drunkenness.

"Get up," was all Gonzalo said, and even in his drunkenness Marcos could tell it was an order and no request.

Gonzalo hadn't seen Elena's body yet, but he hated Marcos at that moment almost more than he had ever hated anyone. He suffered from the frustration of having done all he could in the matter only to witness, finally, all his work collapsed by a drunkard.

Marcos stood and shrugged his shoulders.

"What did I do?" He slurred and in his hand was a bloody kitchen knife.

Gonzalo pulled out his nightstick.

"Drop the weapon!" he shouted.

Marcos seemed not to understand the order and only shrugged again, the knife still in hand. Gonzalo swung the nightstick with both hands, striking Marcos at the wrist with a downward motion. The loud crack made the horse handler give a little jump, and the knife fell to the ground. Marcos doubled over and turned away from Gonzalo, cradling his arm.

"*¡Maldito sea tu madre!*" Marcos yelled, cursing Gonzalo's mother.

Gonzalo walked up behind him and tripped him, making him fall face forward in the grass. He put his knee on the small of Marcos's back and pulled his arms out behind him roughly and cuffed him.

"What did I do?" Marcos asked again.

Gonzalo resisted an urge to slap the back of his head.

"You have the right to remain silent, Marcos. Believe me, anything you say can and will be used against you in a court of law. Don't say a thing until you have a lawyer . . ."

"But . . ."

"Shut up, Marcos. I don't need to hear a thing from you."

Marcos rested his face in the grass and in a few seconds more was asleep again.

Gonzalo really didn't need to hear anything from Marcos. He had the suspect covered with blood and the murder weapon in the suspect's hand. If that wasn't enough, there was the long history Marcos had of beating his wife. If this, along with the pending divorce as a motive, was not enough to convince a jury, then there was Marcos's general surliness when sober, a trait that could not escape a jury. If all this was not enough, there was the fact that an officer of the law had left the suspect and victim alone together and an hour or two later another officer had found them alone together. All these are good reasons why Gonzalo had little interest in hearing the suspect's story. Besides, any good defense lawyer would make much of a statement being taken while the defendant was drunk and without counsel.

Wilfrido Vargas waved from the area near the barn, and Gonzalo called for him to approach.

"Is he giving you any trouble?" he asked.

"Nope. No trouble. He's just falling asleep on me. Take him in to the station house. Don't let him tell you anything. Sit him down in the empty cell and lock him up. Don't leave the precinct for anything, you got that. Not until you get relieved. Don't leave him alone for a second."

"Did you see the body, boss?" Vargas asked as he pulled Marcos to his feet.

"Not yet."

"It's pretty gross. . . ."

"She's a person."

"Oh, I know. I don't mean any disrespect, I—"

"Get out of here, Vargas."

"Yes, sir."

When Gonzalo got back to the Maldonado home, Officers Calderon and Gomez had arrived. They were outside the home with Hector Pareda. Iris Calderon held the infant who was peaceful in sleep; the car seat was at her feet.

"We got Maldonado. Vargas is driving him to town. Anything I need to know about here?" Gonzalo directed his question to Hector, but Anibal answered.

"Hector won't let me inside," he said loudly.

"Good. Anything else?"

"Hey! I'm an officer too. Why can't I go in?"

"I don't need your footprints in there. Anything else?"

"There's no baby milk," Calderon answered.

"Damn it," Gonzalo muttered and he paced away from his deputies and paced back to them.

"Damn it. This is a mess . . . This is a mess. He killed the mother; Marcos is going to jail; that baby's an orphan. Marcos's parents are dead. Elena's father is still alive, but he's a bastard. That baby's a ward of the state now. Either that or he goes to live with Elena's father; he's about sixty . . ."

The baby began to awaken, and Gonzalo knew the first thing on its mind would be food.

"Take the baby to my wife. Mari will know what to do; she'll probably send you to the store; get whatever she tells you."

Officer Calderon crouched to strap the child into the car seat that was its inheritance.

"What are we supposed to do, boss?" Anibal asked.

"We're going to gather evidence."

"But it's open and shut, boss."

"Looks like it, but that doesn't mean we should do a sloppy job. You and Hector should go to the homes around here. Find out if anyone saw or heard anything from this fight. Find out if they know of any fights in the last week or so between Marcos and Elena. Just don't tell anyone Elena's dead. Not yet. I don't need anyone coming here out of curiosity."

"What are you going to do?" Hector asked.

"Examine the crime scene, the corpse. Take pictures . . . Then I have to have a talk with her father. . . . That should be fun. Do me a favor . . . before you go to talk to anyone, get Collazo here. Tell him, I just need him to sit at a crime scene a couple of hours."

Gonzalo turned to go into the house and Hector and Anibal headed towards their squad car.

"Wait a minute." Gonzalo caught their attention. "Did anyone call the coroner?"

"Not me," Hector said.

"Do me a favor. Call them for me. It'll take them an hour or two to find Angustias."

"Sure thing, chief," Hector said, then he got into the car and drove off.

The Maldonado home was quiet and dark and cool. Though it was mid-afternoon, there would be no more direct sunlight hitting the house because it stood in the shadow of several *pana* trees. It was near 90 degrees outside, but the stone floors and walls of the house made it feel no more than 75.

Gonzalo was in no rush to get to Elena's body. He had seen murder victims often enough to know not to expect any mystical insights from being in their presence. Even those killed after a hard and bloody struggle often had a relaxed expression as though the whole affair was someone else's concern and they wanted no more than to nap.

He tried a technique of crime-scene investigation he had seen in an instructional video sent to him from San Juan. He walked into the house slowly, trying to memorize the room, trying to envision the movements of the victim and the murderer in the moments before the crime. The scenario played out in a flash in his mind. Marcos woke, Elena showed him divorce papers, he started hitting her, she grabbed a knife, gave him a nasty cut, he took it from her and killed her. Simple.

Then there was Elena's body on the floor of the kitchen and the small pool of blood around her.

Early in his career, Gonzalo had heard that a cop should never look into the eyes of a murder victim. He tried to remember the reason why. Something to do with a kind of mystical grip on one's soul that a dead person's eyes could exert. Then he had hired Emilio Collazo for a deputy. Collazo had been old ever since Gonzalo could remember, and Gonzalo learned on the job that wisdom had come with his many years.

"Don't be afraid to look a murder victim in the eye," Collazo said. "They deserve it. Anything else is superstition."

Gonzalo looked into Elena's eyes. They seemed to have a small sadness in them, but he couldn't tell whether it had been growing when she died or getting smaller. He shook his head clear of these idle speculations.

"I've got work to do," he told himself.

"If she was stabbed in the chest," he remarked to himself; the sound of his own voice was his only company, "and she fell on her back like this, then how did all that blood spill out of her?"

The knife Marcos was arrested with had a blade approximately nine inches long. Elena was frail. Quite possibly a strong thrust went completely through her thorax, making a hole in her back through which the blood flowed. Gonzalo gently lifted her back a few inches off the floor to confirm this.

"Shit," he muttered. Five of the seven wounds in her chest had come out her back.

He rolled her body a bit further to one side.

"Goddamn it, Marcos," he said.

There were three small chip marks in the ceramic tile beneath her. He was certain these indicated that she was stabbed while already on the ground, Marcos probably straddling her body.

"Crime of passion. Drunken idiot. Can't think straight, can't walk straight, but this, he can do."

The sheriff stood to survey the kitchen.

"Marcos was in here. Nothing else in the house looks disturbed. The whole thing took place here. What was he in the kitchen for?"

There was an open beer bottle on the counter near the sink.

"Makes sense."

He crouched down to the young mother at his feet and looked into her eyes.

"Didn't I tell you not to say anything to him?" he asked. He felt sorry a moment afterwards. "I told you so," was more than useless at this point.

"I could have helped you," he wanted to say. Instead he headed out to his car and retrieved a small camera from the trunk.

Inside the house again, Gonzalo took two pictures of every undisturbed room before heading to the kitchen. Then he photographed the entire room at a wide angle several times before focusing on the victim. He took several photos of the entire length of her body, then several more of her punctured torso, then he crouched and turned her again to take pictures of the wounds on her back and of the chipping of the floor, which he was certain would not show up very well.

When he stood up, Emilio Collazo was standing in the kitchen doorway.

"What's the story, son?"

Collazo was now in his eightieth year, and he had never been one much for small talk. Gonzalo knew that when he asked for the story, he meant the story of the crime as put together so far.

"Elena Maldonado came home with her brand new baby. You know Marcos Maldonado. She was planning to divorce him. I figure she told him, he went after her, she took a knife to defend herself, he took it from her, stabbed her repeatedly even after she fell."

He crouched again to show the puncture wounds in her back and the chips in the ceramic tiling.

"Bastard," was Collazo's response.

"Yeah. We caught him with the weapon, with her bloody shirt. . . . It's pretty open and shut. The only thing that can save him is that he was drunk when I dropped her off here. They might argue he didn't know what he was doing. . . . Get him off with a criminally negligent or manslaughter. Anyway. Not my job to fight that battle. He's going away for a good long while no matter what they say."

Collazo crouched and looked into Elena's eyes then he closed her lids and stroked her forehead gently. He kissed his fingertips and touched her cheek.

"She was a good girl who had a bad life," he said quietly.

"I know. I told her not to tell Marcos about the divorce. She said she wasn't going to . . ."

"Maybe he attacked her for another reason?"

"Could be. Hell, Marcos never needed much of a reason before. . . . He was definitely drunk. . . . I'll get it out of him. I need to get him counsel. I think I'll also need to get him stitched up. He was cut pretty bad. . . ."

"How'd he cut himself?"

"I think she did it to him. Like I said, I think they started to fight, she grabbed a knife, cut him, then he took it from her . . ."

Collazo looked at the body a moment.

"That doesn't look right," he said.

"Well, it's just a working theory."

49

"She's not really bruised. She was feisty. She wasn't about to slash him then hand the knife over. He would have had to pry it out of her hand to get it. . . . There's no bruising on her wrists or upper arms."

"Like I said, it's just a theory. Maybe he did cut himself. He was pretty drunk when I left them. . . ."

"Maybe."

Gonzalo tried to play that scenario in his mind, but it seemed to make little sense. Marcos was right-handed. His right upper arm was cut. That put the knife in his left hand or in Elena's hands or in someone else's hands. Maybe Marcos himself would clear up this small confusion.

"What do you plan to do?" Collazo asked after a minute of silence.

"I've got to tell Perfecto, he's her next of kin."

"He's a bastard too."

"Yeah, but better that I tell him than that he finds out from gossip."

"So all you want me to do is sit here, make sure no one comes in to disturb anything?"

"Yeah. It could be a couple of hours before the medical examiner comes."

"Uh-huh. I brought a book with me. An American Western."

"Good. I'll relieve you as soon as I can."

Gonzalo left the Maldonado home and walked out to his car, thinking how Collazo's reading habits had finally changed from a steady diet of true crime, hard-boiled stories to something a little more in keeping with his usually mild manner. He also tried to think of any other case in their years together where Collazo had resorted to saying a word as harsh as "bastard" twice in one day.

CHAPTER FIVE

Perfecto Cruz was one of those who seemed determined to make his life infinitely more difficult than it had to be. He was deep into his fifties at the time of his daughter's murder, but he looked like he was in his seventies. He had dropped out of junior high school because it didn't suit him, had run off to San Juan, then the navy for two years, then to prison for several years more. No one knew any more what crime he had committed. Certainly no one cared.

He had returned to Angustias at about thirty years of age with meanness written into him. He barged into his mother's house, demanded food and a bed and all the money in the house. The widow had given everything he asked, but that didn't stop him from giving her a shove from time to time, and people suspected worse. No matter. He quickly got into several bar fights with young men he didn't know, and once in Ponce he had knifed a man in self-defense—so he said. By the time he got out of this second stint in prison, his mother was dead and the house he had barged into and the bed he had demanded were all his free and clear. So were an acre and a half of rugged and overgrown property.

His marriage to Elena's mother, also named Elena, was a tragedy waiting not too long to happen. Nobody knew the lady; he had brought her from Santurce. She was thin with yellow hair and clear blue eyes much like the daughter she was pregnant with when Perfecto married her. Years later when Elena was ready for school, many people noted that mother and child were both often bruised. They seemed happy together in those moments before classes began or right after school had let out, however, and it was never the right time to bring up the subject of the bruises while they were smiling. It had been left to Gonzalo to go out to the Cruz home and menace Perfecto with arrest, but Perfecto wasn't afraid, and his wife would sooner have slit her own throat than say a word against a man she knew would sooner or later be back.

When Elena was in the fifth grade, her mother fell out of an avocado tree, breaking her neck. This was Perfecto's claim, and for once Gonzalo believed him, but no one else did. Perfecto was in custody briefly until evidence was gathered and the investigation completed, then Elena was returned to her father's care. On delivering her to Perfecto, Gonzalo had taken him aside and said, "Don't hurt her again." To this Perfecto had replied only, "Get out of my house."

While it was widely reported that Perfecto beat Elena regularly, Gonzalo had only seen evidence of abuse on a very few occasions. Elena, like her mother, had no desire to say a word against Perfecto. When Elena was in her mid-teens, perhaps sixteen, her father stopped beating her, having gotten, some people said, religion. Not that anyone could identify which religion.

This was too little too late to be of value to Elena. After her funeral, someone recalled having asked her how her father was fighting the wilderness of his hillside farm alone. She answered with something less than a shrug and walked away.

When Gonzalo drove up to the Cruz house, Perfecto was nowhere to be found. The house itself was tiny, so Gonzalo merely shouted into it twice. There was no response and no reason to go in.

He cupped his hands to his mouth and shouted into the dense forest. Perfecto hollered back. Gonzalo followed the sound of the voice to a path in the woods. He picked his way carefully and caught sight of a small outbuilding made of rotting wood with a rusted metal roof. This was the toolshed. The area around it was cool and mostly bare due to the dense canopy of foliage above. Here and there were clusters of ferns and some young plants that would never reach maturity because of the lack of sunlight.

"I've got to talk with you," Gonzalo said from about twenty or thirty feet away.

Perfecto stepped out of the shack with a three-foot machete in hand. He had been sharpening it.

"I need to talk with you."

"I haven't done anything, sheriff. If Martinez told you I killed that dog of his, he's wrong. When I was younger, I would have. I'm different now."

"It's not about that."

At the moment, seeing Perfecto with the machete in his hand, Gonzalo tried quickly to think if there was anything he wanted to do less than inform him of his daughter's death. Nothing came to mind.

"I don't know how to tell you this . . ."

At this point most people would have relieved Gonzalo of his burden by begging him to speak, by putting the worst-case scenario in his mouth. Then he could tell them things were not quite so bad. Perfecto waited with disinterest on his face.

"It's about your daughter, Elena."

Perfecto still had no curiosity. Gonzalo understood this. He had often enough reported Marcos beating her. There could be little surprise in another report.

"Elena's dead, Perfecto."

Perfecto looked down to the dirt at his feet and shifted his grip on the machete.

"Was it Marcos?" he asked.

"We think so. He's a little drunk . . ."

"Alcohol turns men into monsters," Perfecto said. Gonzalo agreed.

"Yeah, well, I guess so. It turns out, I think they were fighting and things went too far."

"Fighting?" Perfecto asked as though he had never heard the word.

"Yeah."

"I told her not to fight with her husband. The Bible says . . ." Perfecto stopped and looked at the dirt again.

"She was pregnant, wasn't she?"

"She had the baby yesterday, I think," Gonzalo answered.

"Is the baby all right?"

"Yeah. We need to talk about the baby. Mari is taking care of the child now, but . . ."

"I can't take care of a baby," Perfecto blurted out.

"Well, okay. But is there anyone in the family who . . ."

"I'm the only one Elena had. My wife's family is all dead or they're worse people than I am. Two murderers on that side of the family."

"Okay. We can talk more a little later. I just wanted to give you the news before you heard it as gossip. We have Marcos in custody. Don't worry about him. He's going away for a while."

"Prison doesn't solve problems," Perfecto said. "It doesn't make men good. Trust me."

Gonzalo didn't know how to answer that, so he didn't.

"I'll be back later this afternoon or in the early evening."

"Don't bother. She's dead. I was a terrible father. Talking isn't going to change any of that. Talking doesn't change anything."

Perfecto turned back into his shed, but Gonzalo called him out again.

"Just out of curiosity. When was the last time you saw your daughter, Perfecto?"

Perfecto took a moment to think.

"I gave her a ride home from Colmado Ruiz in my truck a few months ago. Maybe three months ago or four. Why?"

"What did you two talk about during the ride?"

"Nothing much. I asked her how she was doing."

"What did she say?"

"She said she was doing all right."

"Anything else?"

"No. We're not talkers."

"Okay. Just curious."

Gonzalo turned to go, but this time Perfecto called him back.

"Sheriff. When you see Marcos, tell him something for me."

"Go ahead, I'm listening."

"Tell him to repent."

Perfecto went back into his shed, and Gonzalo headed out to his car wondering if he had witnessed in Elena and Perfecto the worst possible relationship between parent and child.

Gonzalo's deputies had started their task of canvassing the area around the Maldonado home. Iris

Calderon had driven out to meet with Hector and Anibal. It was decided that Hector and Anibal would visit homes downhill of the Maldonado home while Iris visited the homes uphill from the crime scene.

Like many homes on the fringes of Angustias, the Maldonado home was surrounded by more wilderness than neighbors. From their front door, no other houses were visible. The nearest home, however, was only across the street and on the other side of a low rise. The lady living there did not get many visitors. She invited Officer Calderon in, gave her a glass of cold Cola Champagne, and wanted to know why she was being visited.

"Did you hear anything from the Maldonado home this afternoon?" Calderon asked.

"Like what?" the lady wanted to know.

"Arguing, a fight, anything like that," Calderon volunteered. Clearly this was already a dead end.

The lady thought hard, biting at the flesh around her thumb.

"Not today," she said.

"Recently?" Calderon pursued.

The lady bit at her thumb again.

"Not recently," she replied. "Do they fight a lot?" she asked.

Iris ignored the question. She wondered how the lady could have missed the violence just a few dozen yards away.

"If you remember anything about anything you

may have seen or heard in the Maldonado home, just call me at this number." Calderon jotted it onto a napkin.

"What kind of noise?" the lady asked. "Did he shoot her?"

"No. Thank you for your time," Calderon said, getting up to leave.

"What happened?" the lady asked, but Calderon kept walking.

Hector and Anibal had better luck with their first interview. The nearest neighbor downhill from the Maldonados was Doña Esperanza. Doña Esperanza was in her seventies and recounted to everyone the hardships she had undergone as a child during the Great Depression. In fact, she often made people feel that her hardships and the Great Depression itself were their fault. Once they had accepted the responsibility for this, she usually went on to make them feel guilty for every other calamity in her life.

Doña Esperanza's house was not much more than a shack built on four cement posts that lifted it a foot off the ground. The house had been built on the inside of a sharp turn, and as it was on a slope, rainwater ran onto her property with every storm, bringing new disaster to her life and digging channels in the red clay in her patio and beneath her home. While it had not rained in several days, the red dirt was soft underfoot so that Hector and Anibal could hardly avoid stepping in mud up to their ankles.

"Don't come in!" she yelled before Hector had even knocked on the door.

Hector, of course, thought she was in some way indisposed. She came to the door, and she cleared up the matter.

"Your feet are dirty," she said.

"Okay. But we need to talk to you. Did you hear anything this—"

"*Mijo*, I've heard just about everything in my life. If I could let you in, I would tell you everything I've heard in my lifetime. *Barbaridades*."

"But have you heard anything this afternoon? Over in the Maldonado house?"

"*Ay, mijo. No me hables de Maldonado,*" she explained. Don't talk to me about Maldonado. "I knew his father. His father was no better. His father was worse."

"But what about today?" Hector insisted.

"Today?" Doña Esperanza squinted. "His father's dead already."

Anibal was frustrated with the interview and took over. "If you don't tell us about what you heard today, I'm going to walk into your house and put my feet up on your table. Talk!"

Anibal made this demand in his usual excited tone, and it took Hector another five minutes of supplication to bring Doña Esperanza back to the door.

"Is he gone?" she asked through the door.

"Yes. Can you open the door?"

"No. You can talk through the door. It's not too hard," she replied.

Hector drew a long breath and glared at his partner who had moved a yard or two away. Anibal returned his look with a smile.

"Look, Doña Esperanza, we are here on very important business. We need to ask you about Elena and Marcos Maldonado. Did you hear anything, a fight, yelling, anything today?"

"Did he kill her?" she asked.

"What makes you think that?" Hector asked, but he did not have the patience to wait for an answer to his questions before providing an answer to hers.

"Yes. He killed her."

"I knew it would happen sooner or later. I guess he finally figured things out."

Hector leaned closer to his side of the door.

"What did he figure out?" Hector asked.

"She was going to leave him."

"She told you this?" Hector was eager over this unexpected confirmation of a possible motive for the crime.

"She didn't tell me anything. I've seen enough pain in my life to tell when more is coming."

"So how did you know it was coming this time?"

"This? This was easy. I knew from the headlights."

"What headlights?"

Doña Esperanza looked up to the heavens as though the case were so plain any person who couldn't understand was another burden placed on her shoulders by God.

"Maldonado has a truck. At night, through the trees, I can see his headlights. He goes to get drunk in Ponce. Sometimes he goes away for hours. Sometimes he comes back the next day. Most likely he has a woman somewhere. There are women who will open their legs for any man, God save me from "

"Doña Esperanza, this does nothing to explain why you think she was leaving him." Hector tried to hurry her along.

"When his headlights go, a little while later, other headlights come. Not a truck. A small car. I hear the car door open and close. An hour or two later, I hear it open and close again, the headlights go on, the car drives away."

Hector stood at the door thinking a moment. Elena seemed so intensely private, it was difficult to imagine her inviting anyone over. Still, she was very young. There again, she was also very pregnant the last few months. . . . He took out a small notepad and a Bic pen.

"Are you still there?" Doña Esperanza asked through the door.

"Yes. I'm thinking . . . Did you get a look at the car? The color maybe, or the number of doors . . ."

"Never saw the car. It's always at night. All I see is the headlights. The truck has high headlights. The other car is lower. That's all I know."

"You never saw or heard the man?"

"No."

"Did you ever talk to her about this?"

"No."

"When was the first time you remember the car coming by?"

Doña Esperanza thought for a moment before answering.

"A few months ago. Maybe three months. I don't keep track of her troubles. . . ."

"When was the last time the car came?"

"A week ago. It was late at night. I didn't see the car come in, I just heard the car door close. It woke me up."

"Around what time of night was that?"

"Midnight, I think. I don't know. I don't stay up that late. I didn't see the car go."

Hector closed his little notepad.

"Thank you, Doña Esperanza. This has been of help. I may come back tonight for a few more questions."

"Make sure it's not too late. I like to go to sleep at ten, before the news."

Anibal wanted to know what had gone on between the deputy and the elderly lady.

"Does she have anything for us or not?"

"I think she may have given us something useful, but Gonzalo will know what to do with it."

"Did she see anything? Hear anything? Did she hear the fight?"

"No, but I think she gave us another motive to work with."

"But what did she say?" Anibal insisted.

"Don't worry about it for now. We have a few other houses to knock on. And another thing . . . If you have another outburst like that, you're staying in the car."

Anibal made no reply to this threat. He tried to convince himself that Hector could never be so cruel, but he wasn't sure he knew his partner well enough yet.

In the Gonzalo home, Mari Gonzalo was struggling to understand the unnamed Maldonado child. The baby would not stop crying though she had already fed him, burped him, checked his diaper, and tried rocking him to sleep. None of this satisfied him, and she was beginning to think the child had already grown accustomed to his mother and missed her. She talked to him.

"*Papito*, this is hard, but your mother isn't coming back for you," she whispered in his ear.

A minute later, she wondered what she was doing talking to an infant and telling him nothing but the most treacherous of truths. She began instead to hum to him and rock him even more violently. This did nothing to stop his crying, and Mari thought he was crying even harder. She sat on the sofa and leaned back, letting the child rest on her breast. It wasn't more than half a minute before he had snuggled his way to sleep.

"Que bandido," she whispered. "He just wanted me to stop moving."

As the child slept, Mari entertained all manner of frightening thoughts. Where would the child go next? What would happen to him? What sort of life would the child lead? How long would it be before the infant was subjected to the cruel coldness of the child welfare agencies? To foster home after foster home.

She wondered if there was anything she could do to interpose herself between the child and the world outside. She wondered why he could not simply stay drawing deep, warm breaths on her chest. She devised schemes by which he could stay with her and her husband. She imagined asking the sheriff if he didn't want to be the father of a boy after three girls. She could not envision a scenario where Gonzalo simply said no to her. She rationalized. After all, she had asked for so little over their many years together. She was still young. She would do all the work.

But that wasn't the way the real world worked, she reminded herself. In the real world, child welfare people came in with forms to be signed, and they took children away, never to be seen again, destined to become a memory one spoke of on the odd morning over coffee. She knew some time not too far in the future she would be turning to her husband at breakfast, saying "Remember the little

Maldonado child . . ." There was nothing, she reminded herself, that she could do to prevent that.

"God, damn that Marcos Maldonado," she prayed. She wondered if it was a sin.

"God, damn him," she prayed again, feeling certain it could not be held against her.

The child made some slight movement in her arms that reminded her he was there. Mari spoke to him directly, whispering with her lips at the crown of his head.

"No matter what happens in this life, you can come to me," she promised him, but even as she spoke the words, she knew they were hollow.

CHAPTER SIX

After informing Elena's father, there was little for the sheriff of Angustias to do but drive into town and begin a preliminary interrogation of Marcos Maldonado. He dreaded this part of the investigation. There was almost nothing to be gained, in his mind. Even a complete confession would be suspect if it came from a man who had passed out from drunkenness just an hour or two before. There was also some question of finding Marcos a lawyer to represent him. Gonzalo had dealt with Marcos before. Marcos was one of those drunks who preferred to sleep, was cranky when not left alone, and talked from a bravado he never displayed while sober. He could yell at the top of his lungs that he killed Elena and was proud of it, and everyone in Angustias would understand it was alcohol making him say more than he should. A lawyer would have to be brought in at some point, probably very early in the interrogation. But who? Maria Garcia was the one attorney in Angustias that Gonzalo trusted, but she had been on the opposing side of the divorce that, in Gonzalo's mind, was the most likely spark to the murder.

Gonzalo tried to figure this all out in the minutes it took to drive from the house of Elena's father to the precinct in the middle of Angustias. There was no easy solution, he decided. The best course was to ask Marcos a few questions first and judge his competency.

The day was sunny and had not yet begun to cool down, and Gonzalo wondered as he parked his car in front of the precinct why the founders of Angustias had decided to put the town plaza on the summit of one of the highest hills in the *Cordillera Central*. Except for a few trees lining the plaza that needed near constant watering, there was no shade in the center of town. He shaded his eyes and looked up, trying to find the sun as he walked to the station house door. He gave up the task as pointless. He knew what the sun looked like, and he knew what it could do.

Inside the precinct, Marrero and Maldonado were in earnest, slurred conversation through the bars that served as a wall between their cells. Officer Vargas was reading the newspaper at a desk.

"What are you doing?" Gonzalo asked his deputy.

"Reading the paper," Vargas answered in an unsure voice.

"But you're letting the inmates talk to each other

freely. Don't. They could be plotting an escape. They could be giving each other alibis. Don't let prisoners communicate if it can be avoided." Gonzalo used a harsher tone than usual, but not nearly as harsh as the voice in his head; that voice wanted to know if Vargas had learned anything at the academy.

"How could I stop them from talking? They're right next to each other. Besides, don't they have a right to—"

"They don't have a right to do anything that could be potentially dangerous to us or help them circumvent justice."

The Angustias station house was one long rectangle, so that from the front door and waiting area, there was a clear view past the desks used by the officers for their paperwork to the two cells. Gonzalo strode past Vargas to the cells in the back and ordered the two men to be quiet. They obeyed instantly but for only a half minute.

"Who does he think he is?" Marrero called out as Gonzalo turned to retrieve a chair for himself.

"He thinks he's some kind of *jefe?* He thinks he owns us?"

Gonzalo ignored the taunt.

"I need to talk to you." He sat outside the cell and addressed Maldonado.

"Don't say anything, Marcos. You got rights. You got a lotta rights," Marrero yelled.

"I want a lawyer!" Marcos yelled.

"You are entitled to a lawyer, but I think—"

"I want a lawyer! You can't keep me here without a lawyer! I want a lawyer!" Marcos insisted. He grabbed the metal frame of his cot and started banging it into the floor for emphasis.

"I'll get you a lawyer."

Gonzalo got up and put his chair back in place. He glared at Vargas as though this uprising was his fault.

"Don't let them talk to each other. If they start that again, throw some water on them," he said in a voice loud enough for everyone to hear.

"*Ay si*," Marrero said. "*Echenos agua. Hace calor.*" Throw water on us. It's hot.

"If they start talking to each other again, bring out the tape recorder," Gonzalo whispered.

Outside in the sunlight again, Gonzalo stood in front of the station house and thought. He didn't want to go to Maria Garcia; he didn't want to go to any of the less competent lawyers in Angustias, and he certainly didn't want to hand the case over to district attorneys and public defenders just yet. He was proud of his ability to put all the pieces of the puzzle together before outsiders started taking over the case, telling him what to do. This interview, as perfunctory as he expected it to be, was a piece of this particular puzzle, and Gonzalo wanted it in place as quickly as possible. Fate took the issue out of his hands.

"Is it true?" The voice startled him.

"Sorry," Maria Garcia said. "I didn't mean to scare you. But is it true? Is Elena dead?"

"Completely true."

"Marcos did it?"

"I've all the evidence I need. . . ." Gonzalo shrugged.

"Are you positive?"

Gonzalo was somewhat taken aback by the question. To this point he hadn't considered any alternatives. He tried to think if he had left any stones unturned in what seemed a simple case. He couldn't think of any.

"Positive. Look. I was going to approach you about this murder sooner or later, probably sooner. Do you mind if we get out of the sun and talk a bit?"

"Come on to my house," she said and walked off to her side of the plaza. Gonzalo followed.

The inside of Maria Garcia's house had none of the grandeur one might expect from the facade. Instead of paintings, she had an eclectic collection of modern prints and rock and roll posters. Prominent was one of the Bee Gees that even Gonzalo knew must have been saved for a very long time. Of even greater prominence on the first floor of the house was a well-stocked bar. Gonzalo tried to think if there were any other single women in Angustias with a stock of rum, whiskey, scotch, and gin in plain sight. He caught himself. After all, he told himself, Maria Garcia was of age to have all the alcohol she liked. Besides, he was sure there were at least a dozen women in town who kept much smaller liquor reserves in hiding places around their homes. That certainly made them no better.

Maria climbed onto a bar stool and kicked off her shoes. After a pause, she prompted the sheriff.

"You wanted to talk to me?"

"Yeah, first of all, we may agree that what happened was a terrible tragedy, right?"

Maria looked like she didn't know what was being asked of her.

"Of course, Sheriff. Did you think I had a reason to think of this as a happy occasion?"

"No, no. Look. Wait. I mean this, this morning, I dropped Elena off here and waited outside a few minutes . . ."

Maria said nothing until Gonzalo felt pressured to say more.

"She told me she was seeing you about a divorce," he continued.

"She was a client. I would prefer not to discuss our dealings at this moment."

"Right. I understand that. I only mention it because I think Elena might have told Marcos of the divorce and that might have set him off, that might have been his motive. Also, I need to interrogate Marcos, and there aren't too many competent lawyers in Angustias. . . ."

Maria Garcia thought a moment. She got off her

stool and walked around to the other side of the bar, pouring herself an inch of rum.

"Want any?" she asked.

"I'm on duty."

"Oh yeah. That makes sense. . . . Look . . . Sheriff. You've put me in a strange situation. What am I supposed to say? Between you and me, she was getting a divorce. She's been planning this with me for a while . . . since she found out she was pregnant. She didn't want Marcos to be involved with the child. I told her, and she agreed, not to divulge her plans to anyone before I had finalized my assessment of the Maldonado holdings, how much we could get, etc. Believe it or not, though a divorce where everyone's happy to get out is a fairly quick procedure, a contested divorce is a long, drawn-out affair. We had every reason to believe Marcos would contest it, if for no other reason than to molest Elena."

Maria took a sip of her drink and chose her words.

"I find it hard to believe that she was able to stay quiet about this for so many months and then just told him when she was alone with him. Especially since there was a baby who could have gotten hurt. I don't think that can be the motive."

Gonzalo thought a moment.

"She told me," he answered. "Maybe she was just tired of keeping it in."

"I don't think so. I saw her this morning. You

know that. She wasn't suicidal, she wasn't talking stupidly. She mentioned she wanted to have everything in place to be able to surprise him and run away. She wanted to wait. If he killed her for this, he found out some other way."

Gonzalo knew Maria's feelings. He knew what it was like to talk to someone who seemed intelligent and have that person go off and do something stupid. He knew what it was like to laugh with someone in the morning who cut their own wrists open at night.

"Well, Marcos is the one who needs representation now. Do you know if there's anyone in Comerio, Narranjito, Aibonito who can do a decent job? I just need to get him through my interrogation. Someone else will get him in San Juan, I'm sure."

Maria thought a minute and picked at one of the buttons of her blouse.

"There's a woman in Naranjito. Carmen Ortiz. She's done a few recent criminal cases. Mostly she does real estate. I think she started as a public defender. She knows the ropes, at least."

"Can you make the call?" Gonzalo asked.

Maria rolled her eyes. She clearly wanted no part in helping Marcos escape punishment. She got up, went to the phone on her kitchen wall and started dialing. She held a conversation in hushed tones, so that Gonzalo was only able to hear that she apologized several times though he wasn't sure why.

Maria hung up the phone and came back to the bar. She finished her drink in a swallow.

"She'll be over in half an hour."

"Good. I'll also need . . ."

"I know, I know. You need a nice quiet place to do the interview, the precinct isn't private, this is an important case, etc. Sure. I understand. The great city of Angustias can once again rent my living room to interrogate a murderer. But this time, I won't be here. I'll call you when Carmen gets here, then I'm leaving."

"I understand. Remember, I'm on your side in this one. I want this guy in jail too. . . ."

"I know, but you don't know Elena. She is . . . was special. She had a strength to her that could have made her useful to a lot of people. She could have been a pillar of any community, but she had to waste her energy fighting off that bastard."

Maria had spoken with such conviction, had put such venom in the last word, that there was little for Gonzalo to do or say. He stood silently a moment and looked at his shoes until the awkward feeling receded and he found himself commenting mentally on the crookedness of his shoestring bows.

"I've got to tie up a few loose ends. I'll be back," he said.

Gonzalo showed himself back out of the house and into the sunlight. He surveyed the plaza from the sidewalk in front of Maria Garcia's house. All was calm. People went about their business or lack of business, children ate *limbels* near the fountain and no one seemed to know or care that someone in town had just murdered someone else an hour or two before.

He walked over to the precinct, avoiding eye contact with the citizens he passed. The last thing he wanted was to be drawn into conversation, and he didn't want to have to answer any questions about why Maldonado was in jail or what he was doing visiting with Maria Garcia. He got to the station house without a single person taking the slightest interest in him.

"The coroner called," Vargas reported from the station house doorway. "He's in Caguas. Won't be able to make it until about four-thirty or five."

"Wonderful. What about the prisoners?"

"They fell asleep while talking to each other."

"What were they talking about?"

"That's the thing. Maldonado was swearing he had nothing to do with it, and Marrero was saying he knew exactly what happened. He said he knew the guy who did it. It was strange, boss. He sounded like he was telling the truth."

"Was he sober?" Gonzalo asked.

"Well, no . . . I mean . . ."

"Then there's your answer. A drunk can say anything. Marrero's a bad drunk; you don't have to pay attention to what he says when he's drunk. Even when he's sober, all he says is bullshit."

"But, he sounded . . ."

"He sounded like a drunk talking about what he doesn't know. Look, if he names names, then write them down. That way we'll be able to show them to the court if Maldonado tries to lay the blame on someone else. Turn on that tape recorder . . ."

"I did; it's all on tape so far. It's just . . ."

"Don't worry about it. Look. I want to meet with Hector and Iris. Wake Maldonado up in about twenty minutes; we're going to have to transport him to Maria Garcia's house."

The drive into the valley where Elena and Marcos had lived was only a few minutes long, but it was enough for Gonzalo to begin reflecting on the enormity of the events of the day. Maria Garcia was right. He had no real idea of how nice or good or strong or weak Elena Maldonado had been. He had no idea what she might have been. Perhaps even worse, there was a child who would never know his mother, probably never know his father.

"*Caramba*," he said to himself as he pulled the car over in front of the Maldonado home.

Collazo was sitting on a metal-frame rocking chair on the porch. Gonzalo called out from his seat in the car.

"Anything?"

Collazo got up and started walking toward the car.

"Like what?" he asked.

"I don't know," Gonzalo answered. "Has anything happened at all?"

"She's dead," Collazo answered. "What could happen?"

Gonzalo gave him a weak wave and continued his drive. Hector's car was only a few yards around the bend, and Hector and Anibal were sitting inside, apparently arguing. Gonzalo parked behind them and leaned in at the driver's side window.

"Any trouble?" Gonzalo asked.

"He thinks someone else killed Elena," Hector said.

Gonzalo stood up and put a hand to his chin as though he were pulling on whiskers he didn't have.

"Who?"

"That's just it. He doesn't have a name. He doesn't have a motive. He doesn't have opportunity. Just the theory," Hector went on.

"Let him speak," Gonzalo answered, and Anibal made use of the freedom.

"I don't think Marcos did it," Anibal said.

"That's it?"

"I think her boyfriend did it," Anibal continued.

"What boyfriend?"

Hector interrupted.

"Doña Esperanza says she saw the headlights of a car come in some nights when Marcos was away. She figures it was a boyfriend. It could have been anyone."

"Do you have anything else? A description of the car? Any other witnesses?"

"We just came from Doña Esperanza's place. We haven't asked anyone else about—"

"Well, start asking. This might be important."

Gonzalo got back into his car and sat there a minute or two as his deputies drove off to the next nearest house. He had not yet stopped to think through the events of the crime in a clear and rational way, and he did not like that a wrinkle was showing. He wanted the case to be open and shut, but he couldn't get it to comply. His own deputies were beginning to find clues that he hadn't thought of. She hadn't fought for control of the knife, she may have had a boyfriend, this unknown man may have played a role; this was like putting a jigsaw puzzle together so that it fit the picture on the box, then finding three or four extra pieces.

He drove to the Maldonado home again, and checked his watch as he got out of the car. Carmen Ortiz might already be in Maria Garcia's house.

"What's the matter now?" Collazo said, getting out of his rocking chair.

"I just want to check something. Come on."

Both men went into the house. Gonzalo headed straight for the kitchen and knelt by the side of the dead woman's head. He opened her mouth and moved his face close to hers.

"What do you want from her now? She's not going to whisper anything to you," Collazo asked.

Gonzalo got up.

"She doesn't have the smell of alcohol in her mouth."

He stepped over the body to the counter where the open beer stood. He looked closely through the dark brown glass.

"This bottle's almost empty."

He looked at the counter around the bottle.

"It was drunk by someone standing right here. See the rings on the counter?" Gonzalo pointed.

"Yup. But so what? I figured it was Marcos that did the drinking. He wasn't too particular about using coasters. That's nothing new."

"No, but this is a tiny kitchen. How long do you think he stood here drinking?"

"He drank pretty fast, I'm sure . . ."

"But still, it took him some time."

"True, maybe two minutes?" Collazo answered.

"Good, now look where she is. She's in front of the door. She trapped him here. The only way he could have gotten out is by going through her. Say they were arguing. Why would she follow him in here?"

Collazo thought a moment in silence.

"Follow this scenario," Gonzalo said. "They argue, he comes in here for a beer, she's still out of this room, maybe in the living room, maybe in the baby's room. They're yelling at each other from a distance. She comes into the kitchen. He's drinking his beer, she's in the doorway. She comes closer, he pulls a knife out of the drawer or from on top of the counter or from the sink. Does she turn away? No. Does she fight him for the knife? No. What does she do?"

"She stands there," Collazo concluded.

"Does that make sense?"

"You're forgetting something," the older man answered.

"What?"

"Maybe he opened the beer after he killed her."

"Hector found him crying in the living room. He was upset; this wasn't cold-blooded."

The two men looked at each other for a half minute, each one thinking.

"Anyway, I've got to go. Keep thinking. I should be back within the hour. If the coroner ever gets here, make sure they take temperatures. Make sure they measure the temperature of the beer too. It might be useful."

"Okay. I still don't see what difference it makes. There was no one else here. If he didn't do it, it was either her or the baby." Collazo smiled at his deduction.

"Not true," Gonzalo said, walking out of the house. "There could always be another person, another motive. Just keep thinking."

Gonzalo got out to his car, and Officer Vargas was on the CB, calling for him.

"What's the matter, Vargas?"

"Maria Garcia has called twice saying I should bring the prisoner over. Apparently she wants to get this all over with. . . ."

"What kind of shape is Maldonado in?"

"He's singing. Can you hear him?"

Gonzalo strained to listen, and just barely made out an X-rated version of the island's anthem.

"Okay, I'll be there in five minutes. Put him in leg

chains, 'cuff him behind his back and walk him to Maria Garcia's house. Keep your hand on his 'cuffs. If he's unsteady, keep your other hand on—"

"I've transported prisoners before," Vargas said. "In the academy."

"Okay, I'll meet you in Maria Garcia's house. Remember, once he's there, don't let him out of your sight for a second; if he goes to the bathroom, you go to the bathroom. Also, all the chains stay on until he's back in his cell. Got that?"

"Got it."

Instead of any official sign-off, Gonzalo heard Vargas say, "Okay, Marcos, let's go bye-bye." Then the CB went dead.

He sat in his car a minute before turning it on. He wondered whether what he had last told Collazo was true or not. "There could always be another person, another motive." He wanted time to think things through, but people were waiting for him in town. He drove back to Angustias still troubled.

CHAPTER SEVEN

"Get up Marcos, and don't give me any trouble."

Vargas walked into Maldonado's cell. There would have been little possibility of Marcos giving the huge officer trouble. Wilfrido Vargas was well over six feet tall and something over 250 pounds and though much of it was fat, a close look at him revealed that there was a substantial amount of muscle. His upper arms bulged in the short sleeves of his uniform shirt. The shirt was about as large as it could be made, but the giant muscles that ran along each side of his spine strained the seams.

Marcos Maldonado was something under six feet tall and weighed a hundred pounds less than the officer. Hard living had shriveled him. His long stringy hair matched his musculature. No second look was needed to see that Vargas could have slung the prisoner over his shoulder and carried him effortlessly. Even in his still drink-dimmed brain,

Marcos knew better than to do anything that might upset the deputy. He pulled up his own pant legs when Vargas stooped to put on leg chains. When they were put on a little too tight for comfort, he said out loud, "You're a big guy," and giggled because the comment had been meant as a reminder for himself.

Vargas locked the cell door with Maldonado standing as close to attention as he could right beside him.

"Where we going?" Maldonado wanted to know.

"To your lawyer."

"I got a lawyer?" Marcos was surprised.

"We got one for you."

Vargas took firm hold of the handcuffs behind Maldonado's back and they started to march out of the precinct.

"Why do I need a lawyer?"

"You'll find out when you meet your lawyer," Vargas answered.

"That guy started it," Marcos mumbled.

The deputy felt a strong urge to get Marcos to say more, but he checked himself. That wasn't his job. If he started Marcos talking without a lawyer, with his lawyer sitting only a hundred yards away, he might jeopardize the case. He might later be called on to repeat Marcos's words, to confirm an innocent plea. Better to leave Marcos to mumble to himself without a reply.

With his free hand, Vargas opened the station house door, and they both stepped out into the sunlight. The sun was beginning its slow summer descent and shone directly in the officer's eyes. He squinted and remembered the sunglasses in his shirt pocket. With his free hand, he put them on, and when he looked up Gonzalo was waving him on from the corner twenty yards away. Vargas gave his prisoner a slight push towards the sheriff, but Maldonado refused to move.

"He started it," he said out loud.

"I heard you the first time," Vargas said. "Don't make me look bad."

He pushed a little harder and Marcos had no choice but to move forward.

"He started it," he repeated. This time he was speaking loudly to someone else, and he was crying.

"I'm not doing anything to you . . . ," Vargas said.

"It wasn't me, it wasn't me! Don't kill me!" Marcos screamed, and he tried to break free from the officer.

Vargas looked up to see his sheriff running towards him, but it was too late. Closer still, coming out from between two cars was Perfecto Cruz. At his side, in his right hand, he held an ax. As Vargas pulled the victim to an upright, standing position, trying to force him to continue the walk to Maria Garcia's house, Perfecto lifted the ax as he would have lifted it to fell a tree. He swung with all the strength of his two hands. Vargas didn't see the result of the swing, but the sound of the ax head wedging its way into Marcos's left shinbone made him jump.

Vargas let go of his prisoner to deal with the threat from Perfecto. Perfecto pulled the ax back again for a second swing. The back swing caught Vargas in the forearm as he was reaching for the weapon. Maldonado fell to the ground, his shin bending forward for a moment, his left foot for a moment still planted on the ground.

Vargas recoiled from the wound he had received, and was a spilt second too late to prevent the next swing. The ax head caught Marcos Maldonado just below the left shoulder blade.

Vargas lowered his shoulder and rammed Perfecto, sending him off his feet and onto the trunk of a parked car. Perfecto rolled off the car and onto the street, the ax clattering a foot or two from his hand.

Gonzalo came close with his gun held tight in both hands.

"Don't move!" he yelled.

Perfecto rose to all fours and eyed the ax.

"Don't move!" Gonzalo repeated.

Perfecto slowly reached for his ax. Gonzalo rushed forward to step on it, but was too late. It was firmly in hand before he could do anything.

"Shoot me," Perfecto said calmly.

Gonzalo took careful aim. He had Perfecto's head targeted.

"Put that ax down, Perfecto. We can work—"

Perfecto put the ax blade to his throat.

"Do what you have to do, sheriff," Perfecto said, then he dug the ax blade deep into his own throat and pulled it across.

"Oh, Jesus," Gonzalo said.

He holstered his gun. He had no idea what it was he was supposed to do. Perfecto toppled over to his side, dropping the ax, clutching his throat. Blood spilled out between his fingers, running freely as though the old man had an overabundance that was in no danger of ending.

Gonzalo moved to get Perfecto to his feet. He put an arm around his waist and a hand to Perfecto's throat.

"Take him to the clinic!" Gonzalo ordered.

Vargas was standing beside his prisoner, clearly confused by what had just happened before his eyes.

"Take him to the clinic!" Gonzalo shouted again. This time the deputy moved. He hoisted the mangled man under one of his arms and carried him to the squad car. At the same time, Gonzalo half carried, half dragged Perfecto Cruz to his car, letting go of the man's throat to open the rear passenger side door and lay him down on the backseat. Perfecto flopped onto his side and began making gagging sounds as though he were trying to cough a fish bone out of his esophagus.

"Hang on there, Perfecto. You're not alone. You'll be okay," Gonzalo told the dying man as he strapped himself into the driver's seat, turned on the car and pulled into traffic.

Vargas was already on the road, his siren and lights on, making a path for Gonzalo.

The trip from the center of Angustias to the clinic was all downhill and riddled with turns so treacherous that the metal and concrete guardrails that lined parts of the road had to be replaced every two or three years because of the cars that occasionally swerved into them. The sheriff was an expert at driving the roads of Angustias and was soon doing more than seventy miles an hour while using his rearview mirror to keep a watch on Perfecto in the backseat as he gurgled his life away.

"Don't die, Perfecto. Don't die. I know why you did what you did. I might do the same if one of my daughters were hurt."

Gonzalo used many soothing words and phrases with Perfecto in the few minutes it took to follow his deputy to the clinic, but there were no words that could keep Elena's father from straightening somewhat with a jerk and coughing a mouthful of blood through clenched teeth. Gonzalo pulled his car into the clinic's parking area as Perfecto ended his many and difficult days with a shudder.

Gonzalo jumped out of the car and went around to the backseat to get Perfecto. Perfecto's still open eyes told him Death had won the race before Gonzalo had even touched him.

"Dammit," the sheriff muttered to himself.

He slid onto the backseat, propping Perfecto's head onto his lap. Dr. Perez came out of the clinic.

"The patient?" he asked with as much excitement as Gonzalo had ever seen in him.

"He's dead," Gonzalo answered.

"No pulse?" Perez asked reaching towards Perfecto's neck to feel for himself.

"No blood," Gonzalo answered.

Dr. Perez crouched at the open door and shined a penlight into Perfecto's eyes.

"Bring him in when you're done out here," the doctor said. He stood up and walked away, putting the penlight back into his lab coat pocket.

Gonzalo swallowed his desire to tell the doctor he wasn't holding this man's head in his lap because it was his job or it was necessary for an investigation. He tried to focus on Perfecto. The thought flashed through his mind that there could be no worse death than to see life ebb away without a loved one near, to lose one's grip on life in the backseat of a stranger's car.

"It didn't have to end this way, Perfecto. You wouldn't have gone to jail for what you did. Not for too long, anyway." Gonzalo tried to comfort the dead man.

"There was no reason to kill Marcos. He was going away for a long time. You could have died of natural causes. You could have lived for your grandson; watched him grow."

Gonzalo smoothed Perfecto's hair away from his

forehead and closed his eyes. He wondered at the dead man's open mouth.

"What did you want to say? What was going to be your final word in life? Were you going to say you were sorry?"

Gonzalo closed the man's mouth, moved himself out from under Perfecto's head and placed it gently on the car seat. It was only then that he noticed that he had sat in a small pool of Perfecto's blood.

"Damn," was all he said.

Inside the clinic, Gonzalo found Deputy Estrada, a white, gauze bandage covering one of his eyes.

"They want to keep me from opening and closing the eye," Estrada said with a shrug.

"What happened in town?"

"Elena's father wasn't too happy about Marcos killing his daughter. He took the matter into his own hands. . . ."

"With an ax?"

"It's what he had. Thank God it wasn't a gun."

Gonzalo moved further into the clinic, towards the examining rooms. In the first one, Deputy Vargas was sitting on an examination table, holding a towel to the cut on his arm and holding his arm in the air as though waiting for some unseen teacher to pick on him.

"You going to be okay?"

"They don't have anyone to work on me. Everyone's busy with Marcos."

"Everyone?"

"That's what it looks like."

Gonzalo moved on to the next examination room. Here, Anna Cardenas had fallen asleep waiting for her father. Her head was resting against the wall at an odd angle; the rest of her body was either slumped against the back rest of the examining table or dangling off the table altogether. Even a slight move could send her to the floor. Gonzalo took off her sneakers and rested her legs on the table, straightening her. Anna turned to her side and curled into a fetal position.

"The only uncrazy one here," Gonzalo whispered.

The sheriff moved to where the most noise was coming from. He walked into one of the recovery rooms. Here Marcos Maldonado's life was in the hands of two doctors and two nurses, and Gonzalo could see the extent of his injuries.

Marcos was on his side. A nurse at his head was monitoring what looked like a box with a couple of small water bottles in it. This was attached to a tube that ran into the patient's back. Some years later, when Gonzalo himself was attached to this machine, he learned it maintained negative pressure to prevent fluids from filling the lungs. The two doctors were working on the wound below the shoulder blade, a nurse assisted them, but Gonzalo could not see that she was doing anything particularly important.

The view of Marcos's leg sent a shiver down Gonzalo's spine, and he took a small step back away from the patient, his prisoner. There were greenish surgical towels placed around the wound as though they were place settings at a dinner. From out of the red and black, the ends of two bones were protruding. The first one was a clean cut, as good as any butcher could have done. The second was splintered. There was a metal clamp holding onto a blood vessel. Another clamp was dug into the wound so the sheriff couldn't see what it was doing, if anything.

Dr. Perez looked up at the sheriff from behind a green surgical mask.

"Can I help you?" he asked. "Are you going to be bringing in anyone else?"

"Hope not," Gonzalo answered. "Is he going to live?"

Dr. Perez shrugged and looked back at the wound.

"I'll be back in a bit," Gonzalo said, but no one paid him any attention.

On his way back to his car, Gonzalo waved for Deputy Estrada to follow him.

"Help me get this guy into one of the examining rooms," he said.

He took hold of Perfecto at the armpits and began to pull him out of the car. Estrada grabbed his legs, and they carried him to an empty exam room, laying him on a table, resting one blood-soaked hand on top of the other. Gonzalo checked Perfecto's pockets, found nothing and left him to rest in peace, closing the door on him.

The two officers got into Gonzalo's car and started off to the station house.

"I know you're hurt. I have a small job for you, but we need a walkie-talkie so you can keep in contact with us," Gonzalo explained.

"What do you want me to do?"

"Just relieve Emilio Collazo at the Maldonado home. Make sure no one trespasses; keep the scene secure until the coroner arrives. Nothing too difficult," Gonzalo answered.

"Can I go home after the coroner takes the body?" Estrada asked.

"We'll see. I assume so . . . If no one else dies today," the sheriff answered and the men continued the trip to the precinct in silence.

At the station, Gonzalo found Hector, Anibal, and Iris Calderon discussing their findings. Marrero was snoring on his cot.

"She had a boyfriend, chief, and I'm sure he did it," Anibal started as soon as Gonzalo had gotten through the door.

"Okay," Gonzalo said holding up his index finger as a sign that the deputy should wait a moment.

He went to the bottom drawer of one of the filing cabinets, pulled out a plastic bag with a fresh uniform, and walked into the bathroom, closing the door on his deputies. A minute later he was out again, the bloody uniform in the bag.

"You guys confirmed the boyfriend?" he asked Hector.

"Yes. Doña Esperanza heard the car come in every so often, at night when she was sure Marcos was out. We still don't have a description. That's the only problem."

"That's the only problem? What if the boyfriend was a woman? What if the car was her father's car? So what if she had a boyfriend. That has nothing to do with her murder, does it?"

"It might," Officer Calderon offered.

"How?"

"Carlos Pedrosa claims he saw the headlights come in several times at night. He lives a couple hundred yards behind the Maldonados. When Marcos pulls out with the headlights on, the light shines toward his front porch. When the other car comes in, it does more or less the same."

"That still just tells us—"

"Wait. Carlos says he knows it's a man. He's sometimes seen the guy's silhouette."

"And is there any connection to the murder?" Gonzalo asked.

No one had a ready answer.

"That's what I thought. Find out if the guy was there today. That would be important. Find out if anyone knows whether Marcos had any idea what was going on in his house."

Gonzalo went to a shelf near the shotgun rack and took down a two-way radio. He handed it to Officer Estrada.

"Relieve Collazo," he said.

Estrada took the radio and left without comment.

"The rest of you can get back into the valley and see if you turn up anything about this mystery man. Remember, if he wasn't there today, he can't be a suspect."

"Where are you headed?" Hector asked, as the four officers were headed out the door.

"I have to be just about everywhere right now. I'm going to make as many visits as possible in one day."

"But where are you headed first?" the deputy persisted.

Gonzalo thumbed vaguely across the plaza.

"Lawyer," he said.

CHAPTER EIGHT

Both Maria Garcia and Carmen Ortiz were standing in the street in front of Maria's house talking with two elderly people. As Gonzalo approached, the elderly people receded at their best speed and the sheriff was certain he knew what they were talking about. They were explaining to the two lawyers how they had seen everything, how they had tried to help, how they had yelled out a warning or had a dream the night before that would have saved the town much heartache if only someone had listened. All this, of course, though they lived several hundred yards from the commotion and upon interrogation they would admit they hadn't really seen anything worth reporting.

Gonzalo slowed down a step, giving the elderly couple enough time to get out of hearing range.

"Let me guess," he said nearing the two lawyers. "They witnessed everything and want to make a full report before *Dios y La Virgin* come to take them to see *San Pedro*."

"They were asking what all the fuss was about," Maria Garcia said.

She tilted her head and eyed the sheriff, who felt foolish.

"What did you tell them?"

"The truth. I don't know. What is the fuss about?"

"We should talk inside," Gonzalo said.

He was rubbing his forehead with the middle and ring finger of his left hand, a sign that a headache was forming. Maria Garcia shrugged and opened the door to her home, letting Carmen Ortiz and Gonzalo in before entering herself. The three seated themselves in her living room, Gonzalo at the edge of his seat with his elbows resting on his knees. He spoke to Carmen Ortiz.

"Your client is in surgery right now. . . ."

Carmen Ortiz was in her mid-forties and wore the uniform of a stereotypical professional woman—a business suit, tasteful heels, hair in a bun, dark-rimmed glasses. There was nothing in her appearance that would suggest to anyone "I'm your friend." Her appearance told the world, "I know my business and you would be wise to stay out of it."

"What have you done to him?" she asked.

Gonzalo had expected an angry reaction, but Carmen Ortiz asked quietly. Her smile, however, told Gonzalo he was in a heap of trouble if his answer didn't suit her. He sensed there was venom in her or that she was already calculating how comfortable a lifestyle Marcos Maldonado would be able to afford once she had done litigating on his behalf.

"I did nothing to him. One of my deputies was transporting him from the precinct to this location. Elena Maldonado's father came at them swinging an ax. I'm sorry to say he hit Marcos twice before he could be subdued. Marcos is in the clinic now being operated on."

"And the man who attacked my client? Is he in—"

"He took the ax to his own throat and killed himself."

"How convenient," Carmen Ortiz said and sat back.

Gonzalo opened his mouth as if to reply, but he checked himself; he couldn't think of an answer that wouldn't cheapen Perfecto's blood.

"Well, Sheriff, before I see my client, I'll want to ask you a few questions regarding the type of care he received and—"

"If you want to take a deposition, you'll have to wait. Believe me, I have a lot to do right now."

"And what do you want me to do in the meanwhile?" Carmen Ortiz asked.

Gonzalo got up and shrugged.

"Maybe you should go see whether you still have a client."

He turned to the door then back again as though he had forgotten his hat.

"Oh, counselor," he said, talking to Maria Garcia. "Did you know Elena had a boyfriend?"

Maria had sat silent and serious throughout the sheriff's interview with Carmen Ortiz. She seemed taken aback by the question. Her face told Gonzalo that she knew about the man in question but didn't think the sheriff would have found out.

"I . . . she was my client . . . attorney, client . . ."

"Sure, I understand. But the neighbors seemed pretty sure about this. If one of them told Marcos . . . You see how it would go to establishing motive."

"Or possibly this boyfriend is the real culprit," Carmen interjected.

"All I've got right now is a rumor, counselor. A rumor goes to motive. If I ever find the man, then we can talk of a second suspect."

With that, Gonzalo went out the door, leaving the two attorneys to have a discussion he hoped would prove fruitful.

Don Justino caught up to him as he walked across the plaza.

"Your little machine, the radio, in the car, it's making noise," the old man said.

"Thanks," Gonzalo replied, tossing the words over his shoulder as he jogged towards the precinct and his car.

"I say again, if anyone is out there, I have a man

down at the Maldonado residence. . . ." Officer Estrada was speaking loudly, but calmly over the radio.

"I've got you," Gonzalo heard Officer Calderon answer.

"I can be at your location in three minutes. Any sign of the culprit?"

"Nope. Just the victim. Elderly male. Collazo."

"I'm on my way too," Gonzalo broke in.

Gonzalo didn't want to hear anything more about the elderly male at the Maldonado home. He was afraid he would have to hear Collazo was injured beyond medical assistance. On the drive to the Maldonado home, he imagined having to hold the old man's hand as his life faded away. He imagined having to break the news to Cristina Collazo, Emilio's wife of sixty years or so. In the movie that played in his mind, it was impossible for him to pronounce the words. It was left for Cristina to come to her own conclusions. The old man had been like a father to him for many years and losing him, Gonzalo felt, would be an incapacitating pain.

When he pulled up in front of the Maldonado house, Officers Calderon and Estrada stood on either side of Collazo, and Collazo sat in the rocking chair on the porch. He was rocking himself gently and holding a wet towel to his forehead. Calderon was holding another towel to the scalp on the left side of his head.

"He needs stitches, but he wanted to make his report to you first," Estrada said as Gonzalo got out of his car.

Gonzalo stepped onto the porch, and Collazo reached out a hand to him. He could see the old man had been beaten soundly, and the hand that was offered to him trembled.

For his eighty years, Collazo was strong, so Gonzalo had not hesitated to bring him in for what was supposed to have been the easy though tedious task of guarding the body of Elena Maldonado. The old man was shaken as Gonzalo had never seen him before. There was a purplish bruise forming under his right eye, and there was dried blood coming from his nose. The skin of his chin was scraped.

"*Mijo*," Collazo mumbled, and by the way he barely moved his jaw, Gonzalo knew it was broken.

"I fell asleep,"

"Forget it. Don't talk. . . ."

"I fell asleep. I woke up. There was someone in the house. In the bedroom. The door was closed. I went to the kitchen. Slowly. Frying pan."

Each word took its toll on Collazo, but Gonzalo didn't interrupt him anymore. He knew it was best to let the story come out. He knew his old deputy would not leave the porch quietly until he had reported.

"I turn around. He punch me." Collazo pulled the towel away from his forehead, revealing a gash three inches long.

"Young, twenty, twenty-five. Thin. My height. *Trigueño*. Dark. Like Clemente. I hit him with the pan." The words slurred out through clenched teeth.

"He hit me, I hit him. I bleed, he bleed. I chase him out. Small car, blue. Toyota. Maybe Mitsubishi. I hit him, he punch me." Collazo pointed to his chin. "I fell."

"Okay," Gonzalo told his friend. "Go now. You need a doctor."

"I go now."

Gonzalo and Estrada walked Collazo to Estrada's car, steadying him as he went. Gonzalo strapped him into the passenger seat. He wanted to stoop over and kiss the top of his head, the old man meant so much to him, but he knew that would not have been tolerated, so instead he smoothed the hair at the back of his head gently. When Estrada was buckled in and the car was on, Gonzalo bent to speak through the window.

"Get him to the clinic. Get Cristina Collazo to the clinic . . ."

"No," Collazo said.

"Okay, get him to the clinic. If he's done getting stitched up, tell Vargas to find me. I need you to make a sweep of Angustias; get on the radio to Comerio, Aibonito, Naranjito. Give them the information we have on this blue Toyota and the beat-up driver."

"Got it," Estrada said, and he put the car in gear.

"And, Estrada, don't lose this guy. We need to

bring him in. If you see him, call for backup, but don't back away. You understand?"

Estrada looked perplexed for a moment and Gonzalo knew he wanted to say, "I know how to do my job." Instead, he nodded, pulled the car out onto the road and sped off, and Gonzalo turned to his other deputy.

Officer Calderon stood on the grass in front of the house, her hands on her slim hips, and she was looking at two twigs sticking out of the ground.

"This is personal now, right?" Calderon asked. She had a bachelor's degree in psychology, and Gonzalo sometimes feared she was making a case study of him.

"It was personal before, deputy. But if you mean is it more personal now, I'd have to say yes. This one won't get away. I guarantee it. Anyway, what are you looking at?"

"The twigs mark a tire track and a footprint," Calderon pointed.

"Good work," Gonzalo said, squatting for a closer look.

"Wasn't me. Estrada may have little personality, but he's a good cop."

"You don't have to convince me. All my officers are good."

"Yeah, but—"

"But what?" Gonzalo stood up and faced his deputy.

"I don't know. You're fair, but . . ."

"Go ahead, Calderon. Believe me, you're not going ruin my day."

"Well, I think you're a little cold toward Estrada. Like he's not really a part of the team. That's all."

To Gonzalo, the accusation seemed to come from thin air. He paused a moment, crossed his arms and tried to think if the accusation had merit. He couldn't figure the problem out quickly, became frustrated, and decided to leave the issue for another time.

"I promise. Once this case is solved, I will try my best to treat Officer Estrada in a manner that makes you happy. For now, I'm going to ask you to let him fend for himself. We have a murder and an assault to solve. Understood?"

Office Calderon straightened herself.

"Yes, sir."

"Good. Now, the guy who assaulted Collazo, tell me about him."

Officer Calderon responded as though this were an academy quiz.

"Well, he's dark-skinned, about five-ten, thin . . ."

"I heard all that. What was he doing here? Who is he? This is the kind of information I need."

"Well, it might be Elena's boyfriend," Calderon answered.

"Might be. But he apparently wasn't interested in the body of Elena. If he was Elena's lover, I would expect him to be crying, not punching an old man. This man was a thief. But of what?"

"I saw the bedroom. It didn't look touched." Calderon said this as Gonzalo was headed to the door of the house.

Inside the house, Gonzalo went straight for the bedroom. A quick survey showed it to be immaculate. The bed was made, the closet door closed, the drawers of the bureau shut. On the bureau there was only the normal paraphernalia—hairbrush, perfume, deodorant, makeup items, a small jewelry box Gonzalo opened with the tip of his pen. The box had several gold rings of various designs, three thin gold bracelets, two pairs of gold hoop earrings, and three twenty-dollar bills folded.

Gonzalo paused to think of the options.

"If he had taken something large, he wouldn't have been able to hit Collazo so easily," he said out loud.

"What if he didn't find what he was looking for?" Calderon asked. "Maybe Collazo interrupted him before he could really start to look."

Gonzalo nodded, but Calderon could tell he wasn't thinking of what she had said.

"Someone knows who this guy is and that someone is going to tell me." Gonzalo said this walking back out of the house. Officer Calderon followed him closely.

"Who knows who this guy is?" she asked.

"I don't know. Somebody. Marcos. Maria Garcia.

Somebody. I'll start with the lawyer. Stay with the crime scene until you're relieved."

"What if the coroner picks up the body?"

"Stay with the scene. If the guy comes back, arrest him."

"If he gives me trouble?"

"Shoot him."

Gonzalo got into his car.

"If you have to shoot him," he yelled out of the window, "shoot him in the legs. Just don't hesitate, that's all."

Officer Calderon went back into the house and surveyed the front room carefully, trying to reconcile the little she knew from Hector's report with the bits of evidence left behind. There were the drops of blood near the sofa where Marcos had been found sitting. There was still an indent in the plastic covering on the furniture where Marcos had been sitting. There was blood on that as well. She tried to envision his exact position.

In her mind, he sat in a dejected state, as many prisoners sit in prison when they begin to feel what they have done. His elbows rested on his knees, blood dripped from his elbow forming a neat drip pattern on the floor below. She carefully examined the rest of the floor, squatting for a closer look.

Two feet away from the sofa, there was more blood. A splattering like a house painter makes when cleaning brushes. A foot further from the sofa and there was more blood, now smeared somewhat. It seemed as though Marcos had thrown the knife then scrambled to pick it up.

She wondered whose blood was slashed across the floor.

"If it was Elena's, then she was stabbed here and ran to the kitchen where he finished her," she thought, but that didn't seem to make sense. "If I was stabbed here, I'd run towards the door, not further into the house."

The mystery soon solved itself to her satisfaction. The splattered blood was a part of Marcos's defense. He slashed himself as he sat, hoping to show that Elena had attacked him, that the murder was really no more than self-defense. He dropped the knife in pain. Hector came in, bandaged him, and when he went to check on Elena in the kitchen, Marcos picked up the knife and ran. At the moment, this scenario seemed reasonable to Officer Calderon so she moved on.

She went into the bedroom to examine it more closely than she had done before. Again, a quick survey revealed nothing out of place. She wandered through the room, her hands in her pockets, careful to touch nothing. She studied the night table and the bureau for evidence that any of the objects on them had been moved.

Elena had not gotten around to dusting the house in the time before she was killed. Marcos, of course, had not even thought of dusting, so there was a film of dust on every piece of furniture. Still, there was no evidence that anything had been moved. The clothes she had worn home from the hospital were lain across a chair near the closet. Her shoes sat under the same chair, neatly arranged side by side. All seemed normal, but then what was normal for the bedroom of Elena and Marcos Maldonado?

Calderon decided that it could not much hurt the trail of evidence if she used a pencil to pull the bureau drawers open and merely looked in at the surface for signs of disturbance. But that done, there was nothing in the drawers that seemed out of the ordinary. She went on to use the same pencil to open the closet door. She studied every article of clothing, going so far as to pry open the pockets of a couple of blazers, but it was useless. Worse than useless, it was a waste. After all, while large items like televisions and VCRs left an almost palpable void, the thief had clearly not taken anything large. The disappearance of a small item would only be noticed if the detective knew what should be in the room in the first place. Even Marcos Maldonado might have a bad time trying to figure out what had been taken.

Officer Calderon decided to move on to the kitchen. There was still the body of Elena lying quietly on the floor. The pool of blood oozing out from underneath her was drying. Her hair was still splayed out across the tiles. On the counter, the beer had warmed, the condensation had puddled and dried. Calderon felt an urge to open the refrigerator door and see if there was another beer. Of course there had to be another beer, probably a whole case. Marcos was a notorious drunk, and all of Angustias knew he had been celebrating the birth of his child since the day before Elena had been driven to the hospital by a neighbor. Still, no matter how much she wanted a beer, no matter how many beers there were in the refrigerator, no matter how cold those beers were, Iris Calderon would not go so far as to take one. After all, they weren't hers. Besides, Elena's leg was in the way—the door could not be opened without moving the limb.

"Damn," Iris said softly to herself. "I've got to sit with a dead body on a hot day, beers sitting in the fridge, and I can't get one. That's got to be what hell is like."

Iris walked out of the kitchen and back out onto the porch where she stood and wondered at what point in her life she had learned to care more for beer than the tragedy encountered in human life; at what point had she learned to be disrespectful of the dead.

CHAPTER NINE

What wasn't on Gonzalo's mind as he drove out of the valley that defined half the territory of Angustias County? So far that afternoon, there had been a murder and a suicide. The murder case seemed fairly simple, but complications were arising, foremost among them was that the suspect might not survive the day having been hacked with an ax while in custody.

The picture of Perfecto swinging into Marcos's shinbone sent a shiver down Gonzalo's spine. The idea that an orphan newborn was in his wife's hands sent another chill through him. He had a vision that she might ask him to adopt the child, but he cast it out of his mind and concentrated his energy elsewhere.

"Who attacked Emilio and why?" he asked himself.

Of course, the possibilities were endless. People were drawn to crime scenes. If the guilty party always returns to the scene of the crime, it's probably because everyone else is headed there. That's why Collazo was there in the first place—to keep the curious away. Maybe it really was just a thief, someone who heard of the Maldonado murder and figured they might be able to find something of value while Marcos and Elena were indisposed. But for reasons he couldn't figure out, Gonzalo discarded these possibilities. It was clear to him that the intruder was Elena's boyfriend. He had no evidence to lead him to this conclusion; he was relying on his gut.

"That's not a good thing," he told himself. "If you keep going this way, soon you'll be using a rabbit's foot and going to an *hechicera* to have her tell the criminal's name from her crystal ball."

He tried to remind himself that he was hired to apply his brains to cases, not his instincts, and that jumping to conclusions wasn't going to solve anything.

Gonzalo parked in front of the precinct and walked across the town plaza to Maria Garcia's house. He knocked, but there was no answer.

"*Se fueron.*" Don Justino had made his way close to Gonzalo's elbow without being noticed and scared the sheriff.

"When did they leave?" Gonzalo asked.

"A few minutes ago. What kind of detective are you, always asking me questions? Don't you know anything that goes . . ."

"Do you know where they went?"

"To eat, I think." Don Justino lifted his cane and

pointed it in the general direction of Cafetin Lolita, the only traditional eatery left near the plaza.

"Thanks," Gonzalo said and started walking away.

"The new priest wants to see you," Don Justino called out.

Gonzalo turned.

"How do you . . . ," he started to ask, but the old man was holding his cane out, pointing in a different direction now.

Alberto Moreno was not really new to Angustias. He had been working in the town for a half-dozen years, but it was only in the last year and a half, with the death of Father Perea, that he had taken full responsibility for the souls of Angustias. Many of the older citizens had loved his predecessor, and felt Moreno was something of an intruder. He was in his thirties, tall, thin, and handsome with a full head of wavy, black hair combed over to one side. To some eyes he looked more like a playboy than a priest. The fact that he often did not wear the uniform of his profession, instead going about in jeans and cotton rugby shirts, did nothing to add to the tremendous authority he could have enjoyed if people could only take him seriously.

Father Moreno jogged across the plaza, making a beeline for the sheriff. Don Justino was just fast enough to walk away without having to greet him.

"Sheriff, I'm glad I caught you. I know you're busy, but I need to ask a couple of questions, I wonder if you have the time."

"I can spare a minute but really no more than that, Father."

"That's all I need, I think. I heard Perfecto may have . . ."

Father Moreno stopped at this point, grimacing as though his facial expression would finish his sentence for him.

"Killed himself," Gonzalo finished the sentence. "Yep. No one ever committed suicide more completely than Perfecto. Anything else?"

"Did you witness the event?"

"The event? Yes. He drew a blade across his own throat and bled to death within a couple of minutes."

"Was he in his right mind? I mean . . . Do you think he knew what he was doing?"

"I can't say. That's not really my area, Father. You understand. But I think I know your real question. You want to know if you can bury him, right? Well, let me tell you, Perfecto led a life full of sin and ended it with sin. My guess? I think he felt guilty about the way he had treated his daughter and took it out on himself. Well, Marcos and himself. Save yourself the trouble, father. Besides, I think he converted to Methodism or something. He's their headache, if they care. Anything else?"

"Yes, just one more thing. There was a child, no?"

"Elena's baby, yeah. Why?"

"Does the child have any family, relatives it can go to?"

"I haven't done a full search yet. My best guess

right now is no. Elena's side of the family is more or less worthless as far as I know."

"And Marcos's side?"

"Extinct. I might be able to find someone, but not right now."

"Well, I just want you to know that the Church stands ready to help the child. I know some people in San Juan. We can work to place the child with a good family."

"If it comes to that."

"Exactly. Of course, it's better if you find family, even Methodists."

Father Moreno said this last with a smile, and the thought flashed across Gonzalo's mind that the people of Angustias might warm to the priest in another few years when his looks had faded a bit and his hair had grayed.

Cafetin Lolita was a holdover from days when those who ate outside of the home were all adult males who worked somewhere in the center of town. Decades earlier, when Lolita Gomez started her business, it had never dawned on her that school-aged children would one day be given money and the freedom to choose their own meals. Nor that women would one day have jobs in town as well and want a place to eat. The difference between Lolita's customers and the customers at other eateries near the plaza was that the people who came to Lolita's diner wanted a full hot meal and the time and quiet to eat it peacefully. Those in the pizza parlor or the fried chicken place wanted to be done with eating even before they had ordered their food, and they didn't want quiet and they didn't want peace.

Lolita Gomez was perhaps seventy years old but was still coy about her age and just about everything else. She had no printed menu and wouldn't tell anyone what was in her dishes. In her mind it was no one's business what was in the food as long as it tasted good, and in her decades of cooking, no one had complained that her food did not taste good.

When Gonzalo walked in, the only customers were the two lawyers at one of the four tables in the diner and an elderly man eating a bowl of rice soup with a piece of bread.

Gonzalo pulled out a seat at the table with the lawyers without asking for permission, and they stopped talking to each other and focused their attention on the sheriff.

"Is there something you want, Sheriff?" Maria asked.

"The name and address of Elena's boyfriend," Gonzalo spoke plainly.

"Is there a good reason why I should break a confidence I had with a former client?" The lawyer countered with a tone that suggested she was inclined to resist him in this point.

"You remember Emilio Collazo? He was my deputy for a while."

"Of course, I remember him, but I don't see—"

"I deputized him again to sit in the Maldonado house until the coroner arrived. Standard practice. Keeps curious teenagers away. Well, somebody decided to enter the house anyway. They beat him up. We think they stole something, and I think it may have been Elena's boyfriend."

Maria Garcia sat silently for a moment, her forkful of salad waiting patiently in midair to be carried higher or brought back to the plate. Carmen Ortiz looked steadily at her plate and moved peas about with her fork.

"I need the name of this guy."

"I can't do that just yet. I've got to think a little . . . Maybe this evening. . . ."

"I need the name now, Maria. For all I know, this guy is leaving the country. You're only helping him to get away with assault, who knows, maybe murder too. . . ."

"Pressuring me isn't going to get you anywhere. I have responsibilities. I'll talk to—"

"Responsibilities? To who? Elena's dead. She's not coming back to you, counselor."

"But what about the child, Sheriff?"

"What about the child?"

"Do you know who the father is? Does it belong to Marcos? Does it belong to Elena's boyfriend?"

"What difference does it make? If that child's father committed a crime, any crime, I'm putting him away."

"There's a big difference. Right now, Marcos is

the father; the boyfriend is a rumor. Marcos is at the edge of death. If he dies, the boy inherits Marcos's property. Hell, he probably inherits Perfecto's land too. I'll have to look into that. If he's not the son of Marcos Maldonado . . ."

"Then he gets nothing from Marcos. So?"

"Easy for you to say that. Do you have any idea how much land Marcos owns?"

"Four or five acres. It's overgrown and hilly. Almost worthless. Maybe a thousand dollars an acre . . ."

Maria Garcia ate her forkful of salad, took a sip of her Coca-Cola, and smiled.

"Nope. Not even close. Look, this is public information, so I'll save you the legwork. When Elena came to me about a divorce, I started searching to find out what we could get from a division of Marcos's property. When I started I thought like you did, a few acres, a beat-up pickup truck. Half of nothing is nothing. But that's what he has in Angustias."

She took another forkful of salad, dipped it into a tablespoonful of dressing that sat on her plate and ate it.

"So what does he have, a Texas oil field?" Gonzalo asked, hoping to speed up the story.

He wondered why so many witnesses with valuable information tried to drag out their disclosure as long as possible. He gave Maria the benefit of the doubt that she might actually be hungry.

"He has, through no fault of his own, forty-nine acres, *llano*, along the *numero dos* going into Isabela."

Maria took a sip of her soda, and Gonzalo knew it was for dramatic effect. Still, the news was worth being dramatic over.

"What do you mean 'along the *numero dos*'? What do you mean *'llano'?*"

"*Llano* means 'flat,' Sheriff. As flat as this table here. Perfect for construction. I've gone out to see it. You can play pool on it if you want."

"And along the *numero dos* means . . . ?"

"It means what I said. Eight of those acres are directly on the Number Two Highway. It leads right into Isabela. You could put a gas station, a rest stop. You could put a whole mall on his property. Or you can make a residential community with half-acre lots. It is prime real estate like you don't find in Puerto Rico anymore."

Maria sliced away a piece of chicken breast and put it into her mouth. She gathered yellow rice and peas onto her fork as she chewed. Gonzalo waited for her to finish with the mouthful while he tried to guess how much money this meant for the Maldonado child.

"How much money are we talking here?"

Maria swallowed.

"Low figure? One hundred and forty thousand."

"Impossible," Gonzalo let slip. "Marcos Maldonado was sitting on one hundred-and-forty-thousand dollars and he didn't leave town, he didn't go on a spending spree, he didn't gamble it all away? That's hard to believe."

Maria Garcia took another sip of her soda.

"He doesn't know how much he has. Hell, Sheriff, he might have forgotten. He inherited the land a few months ago. So far as I can tell, he got a telegram telling him he had inherited such-and-such an amount. Elena says a lawyer came over, gave Marcos some paperwork, had him sign a few documents, and Marcos got drunk complaining that he didn't have time to deal with the four and a half acres he already had. He never went to see the property. Doesn't want to know about it. Frankly, I don't really want him to know about it either. . . ."

"Why not? A hundred and forty thousand might make him a new man. He might even get himself a new suit. . . ." Gonzalo laughed at his image of Marcos in a suit, but Maria Garcia was stone-faced.

"It's one hundred and forty thousand per acre, Sheriff. Per acre. As a low figure, the entire property is worth about seven million dollars."

Gonzalo was speechless for a moment. For a second he tried to do the math in his head. For a few seconds more, he indulged in the fantasy of what he would do with an inheritance like that.

"What's the high figure?" He asked.

"About eleven million."

"Where'd it come from? No one in his family ever had that much money."

"You're right. No one had that much money, but a great-aunt on his mother's side died, and that side of his family has had the land since long before there was a *numero dos*. The land has appreciated. The government is thinking of expanding that highway. The value of the land could go up. If they curve the highway, put a shoulder, whatever, they could get another quarter acre or a half acre more of frontage." Maria shrugged.

"You can see why I have to be extra careful before I give you any information that might jeopardize the child's chances of obtaining a fortune."

"But he's not your client. . . ."

"Sheriff, it's not ethical for me to walk away from the boy because his mother's dead. Trust me, not many others are going to look after the boy's legal and financial well-being."

"But . . ."

"No buts, Sheriff. Now let me eat in peace. I'll be going back to my house in a few minutes. I'm supposed to get a call back from Judge Negretti in San Juan in another half hour or so. I'll discuss the case with him. If he tells me to give you the name of the boyfriend, you'll get it. Meanwhile, if Marcos dies or if he looks like he's going to pull through, it will affect the case, so please keep me informed."

With that Maria Garcia devoted her full attention to the plate in front of her.

Carmen Ortiz looked up at the sheriff as he got up to leave. Her look told him that she too was a prisoner to Maria's scruples but that she thanked him for introducing the element of reasonable doubt into her case.

CHAPTER TEN

Gonzalo went into the precinct and locked the door behind him. Marrero was still snoring softly, lying facedown on his cot mattress. Gonzalo rolled the windows shut so that the station house took on a twilight appearance. He sat at his desk and put his face into his hands.

If there was anything Gonzalo was proud of, it was his ability to think clearly and to follow a logical train of thought through to a logical conclusion. That very week he had told his wife that he wished he had more difficult cases to solve. He told her he was bored of settling the occasional domestic dispute or breaking up Friday-night fights at Colmado Ruiz or searching for goats that had eaten through their leashes. Now that he had a difficult case, he wished it would go away.

That a new mother would be stabbed to death the very day she brought her baby home from the hospital was a shock. That Elena had a boyfriend, that the baby may not have been Marcos's child, that Marcos was worth millions of dollars. All these were shocks. That Perfecto Cruz would come after someone with an ax before his very eyes, that Perfecto would slit his throat before his very eyes, all of this was shocking. That Collazo would be beaten while on the most routine mission, this was shocking as well.

That he could not see a pattern to all this was most shocking of all.

"You're assuming all these events are related," he said to himself out loud.

He started to wonder how he should pursue the case if the beating of Collazo and the murder of Elena had no connection.

Then the phone rang.

"I need you to bring me some formula and some clothes for the baby," Mari said before Gonzalo had finished saying "Angustias Police."

"Is it an emergency yet?" he asked.

"What do you mean? The baby has to eat. I need to give him a bath. He needs more clothes."

"I mean do you need this right now? Can it wait an hour or two?"

"Let me check how much formula he has left."

Mari put the phone down, and Gonzalo listened to her track into the kitchen, open the refrigerator, close it and come back to the phone in the living room.

"I think you have about two hours. Do you need

me to call one of the neighbors? How are things going?"

"Collazo got beat up while waiting for the coroner at the Maldonado home."

There was silence on the other end of the line for a moment.

"Is he going to be okay?"

"You know him. He's strong. He's in the clinic getting a few stitches. The worst part is going to be explaining this to Cristina. It was supposed to be a routine job."

There was silence for an awkward moment again.

"If Marcos is in jail, who beat up Collazo?" Mari asked.

"Good question."

"I mean . . . Marcos didn't have a partner in killing Elena, right? He did that by himself, right?"

"That's another good question."

"I mean . . . Whoever went to the house wasn't there to mourn Elena, right? They were there for something else, right? Maybe even to steal, right?"

"Very good questions," Gonzalo answered.

"Well?" Mari asked, and Gonzalo knew she wanted to hear some of his answers.

"We think Elena had a boyfriend. . . ."

"You're kidding."

"We think it was the boyfriend who came in and took something—we don't know what yet—and when Collazo caught him, he fought his way out of the house."

"What did he take?"

"I have no idea. It could have been something as small as a ring he gave her or a letter he sent her."

"Are you sure he took something?"

"Nope. He might have been still looking for it when Collazo interrupted."

"No. I mean how do you know he wanted to take something? Maybe he was putting something into the house."

It was Gonzalo's turn to be silent.

"Is that possible?" Mari asked.

"I guess so . . . Look, I've got to get back to work. I have to go see Collazo and Marcos. I have to take a good look at that house. I'll try to get over to the house with the formula and any clothes I find for the baby. Love you."

"I love you too."

Gonzalo sat in the quiet of his station house, trying to think through what sort of things Elena's boyfriend might want to leave behind so desperately that he'd risk going to prison.

"Was that your wife?" Marrero asked.

The sheriff was startled by the prisoner he had forgotten. Instead of answering, he got out of his chair and left the darkness of the precinct and headed for his car.

He drove off, heading for the clinic, but came across Hector and Anibal as they were headed into town. Hector flagged him down, flapping his arm against the side of his squad car. Gonzalo pulled over onto the grassy shoulder of the road, and Hector made a U-turn and pulled up behind him. The three officers met on the grass between the cars and stood with their arms crossed.

"What do you have for me?" the sheriff asked.

"Another rumor," Hector responded.

"What?"

"The boyfriend drives in from La Cola."

This information caught Gonzalo by surprise. La Cola, the Tail, was the least developed barrio of Angustias. The neighborhood, if it could be called that, sat on the top of the highest hill in Angustias, a road having been paved through the dense forest twenty or thirty years earlier. At that time there were plans for houses to be built along with a store or two, and there was hope that a community would develop. But the hill was very steep. The electric company refused to make more than a vague gesture at providing power to the area. The water company put up a mile or more of pipe only to find that the fight against gravity was too great and no more than a trickle would come out of a faucet at the top of the hill.

Still, several families had torn a living out of the hill. With the exception of a photographer who only spent a fraction of the year living in La Cola, the rest of the inhabitants were the poorest in Angustias. They were also, by and large, the least educated. For these reasons, La Cola, the Tail, was often referred to as *El Culo*, The Ass.

"Who says he came from La Cola?"

"Doña Amelia. She says she saw the car in front of the Maldonado home a couple of times, a blue Toyota. She saw the same car come down from La Cola once. That's her info."

"Did she describe the driver?"

"Roberto Clemente is what she said."

"So we're definitely talking about the intruder who beat up Collazo."

"There's more, chief." Anibal could not contain himself.

"She said the driver had a companion the last time she saw the car. He was riding in the car when she saw it come off the hill. She was a little confused about specific facial features, but she said he looked like the guy's little brother."

"But did she know these guys? I mean, I don't know anyone that looks like Clemente, certainly not any brothers that look like that in La Cola."

"She didn't recognize them," Hector answered. "But it wouldn't be that hard to hide in La Cola. There's a dozen roads that break off the main one up there. All of them lead to at least one other road. On each path there's a house or two that has been abandoned for years."

"So that's what we have to do. We have to go up there and go to each abandoned house. They must be up there some place."

"You want us to get started on that?" Hector asked.

"Let me think a second. Go to Colmado Ruiz and get yourselves something to eat."

"We can do the search without stopping for . . ."

"Right now, I don't want you to do the search. These guys could be murderers; until we get a little more information or a little more manpower on the road, I just want you two to stake out the exit from La Cola. Get some food and wait for them to come off the mountain."

"What are you going to do, chief?" Anibal asked.

"I'm headed to the clinic. Hopefully, Wilfrido is stitched up by now. I'll radio you from there. Watch that hill," the sheriff tossed over his shoulder as he walked to his car.

Gonzalo continued on toward the clinic. He was greeted by Dr. Perez in the lobby.

"The coroner called."

"Why?" Gonzalo's voice was filled with the annoyance that came from a long day gone bad and the knowledge that the coroner had called to say he wasn't coming.

"He's not coming. There was a body found in the trunk of a car in Coamo."

"Let me guess. He wants us to take pictures, bag the hands, and get the body to him."

Dr. Perez nodded.

"How's Marcos?"

"He'll live. He's sedated now, but it'll wear off in an hour or so."

"And Collazo?"

"Resting. Seven stitches. He'll need bed rest a few days. He's worried about his crops, avocados, I think."

"I'll get them for him. Has Vargas been stitched up?"

"He's in with Collazo," the doctor said nodding.

Dr. Perez walked away and thumbed towards one of the rear exam rooms. Gonzalo headed down the corridor of exam rooms and offices and found his old friend sitting in a plastic chair, his hands folded in his lap. Officer Vargas was leaning against the wall across from him, his good hand behind his back, his other arm dangling at his side carefully bandaged.

"What are you two doing loafing here? There's work to do." Gonzalo tried to make this sound funny but failed. To Collazo he sounded sad. To Vargas he sounded stern. The deputy straightened, almost coming to attention.

"The doctor told us we should wait here and rest a little. I feel fine . . ." Vargas began to protest.

Gonzalo held up a hand.

"I was joking," Gonzalo said, but Vargas didn't know how to react and the moment became even more awkward.

"Wait for me outside."

Vargas left the room and was glad. Gonzalo sat next to his former deputy.

"How are you doing?"

"You don't have to worry about me. I've been through worse."

"I'm not worried about you. I'm more worried about Cristina. Have you spoken to her yet?"

"Not yet. Soon, though."

"Do you want me to tell her about what happened?"

Collazo looked at Gonzalo sideways and smiled.

"You want to tell my wife about how I got beat up by some young *teasto*? Why?"

"Well . . . I don't really want to tell her about any of this. It was a terrible idea on my part to bring you in on a murder. I just thought the murderer was in jail already."

"You have nothing to apologize about, son. I'm old enough to make my own decisions. I decided to work for you today, nobody else did. I fell asleep; I came after the guy in the house. I could have pretended I was still asleep . . . Don't worry about my wife. I'll tell her. It's my responsibility, not yours."

Gonzalo patted Collazo's knee a couple of times and got up to leave.

"If you need anything, let me know."

"Where are you rushing to?"

"I got a tip about where your Roberto Clemente has been hiding himself. I'm going to see if I can bring him in today. Don't worry. The guy who did this to you is as good as in chains."

Gonzalo gave a wave and left the room, closing the door behind him.

"You think too much," Collazo said to the closing door, but the sheriff didn't hear him.

Walking out towards the waiting area again, Gonzalo passed the exam room where little Anna Cardenas was lying listlessly on a paper-covered exam table. He took a step back, opened the door and poked his head in.

"Where's your father?" he asked.

Anna shrugged.

Gonzalo continued on to the waiting area and found Officer Vargas. He explained about the Roberto Clemente look-alike in La Cola.

"I want you to drive Anna home first. Make sure her father's there. Make sure she gets to bed. Then get yourself something to eat. I need you to join Hector and Anibal. I'll radio you guys in a little bit."

"What are you going to do?" Vargas asked.

"I've got to call the funeral home so they can pick up the body."

Officer Vargas escorted Anna out to his patrol car. She said nothing at all when he told her he was taking her home, and she was silent even when her father waved from the field where apparently he had forgotten all about her.

Gonzalo, meanwhile, made a phone call to Pablo Santoni. Santoni owned the only funeral home in Angustias. His was the only hearse, and he had the only facilities for preserving the dead, and he had often done work for the city.

"What do you want me to do?" he asked. "Keep her for you a while, or transport her to Ponce?"

"I need you to take photos and transport her to Ponce."

"Will I be doing the funeral?" Santoni asked.

"I haven't looked for her family. Right now, all I can say is that my best guess is that Angustias will pay for the burial. That could change."

Santoni promised to be at the Maldonado home within the quarter hour.

Gonzalo went out to the Maldonado home. Officer Calderon stepped off the porch and went over to his car as he headed for his trunk.

"What are you up to?" she asked as he opened the trunk.

"This," he said holding the plastic bag with the murder weapon in it.

He marched into the house, headed straight for the kitchen, stepped carefully around the body of Elena Maldonado and opened a drawer under the counter. He closed it after a glance and opened each drawer and cabinet door in the kitchen one by one, closing each one in turn.

"What are you looking for?"

"I'm looking for a match. I should have done this as soon as I came in the first time. This knife doesn't look like any of the others."

"So it came from outside," Calderon concluded.

"Which means . . . ?"

"Which means Marcos didn't kill her."

"That's a good guess, Deputy. It's beginning to look like Clemente did more than just attack Collazo."

The two officers stood in the kitchen for a full minute.

"But can you prove Clemente had the knife? Can you prove it was him?"

"In an hour or two, Marcos will be ready to talk. He'll corroborate. But we have better evidence than that."

"What?"

"Well, we probably won't be able to get useful prints from the knife . . . everyone has handled it because we thought we had caught Marcos red-handed, but . . ."

"The bottle on the counter?"

"Yep. If it wasn't Marcos drinking from that bottle, if it wasn't Elena, it was Clemente. I'll just take it for safekeeping."

"Sure, but boss . . ."

"What?"

"Well, two things. First, you have to catch Clemente . . ."

"That goes without saying. What else?"

"It's a long way between drinking a bottle of beer and stabbing someone to death. The bottle is just evidence that he was here. How are you going to—"

"Leave all those details to me," Gonzalo said.

A few minutes later, the sheriff of Angustias was packing the bagged knife and the bagged bottle in the trunk of his car. He radioed Hector.

"I'll be over there in a few minutes, maybe a quarter of an hour. I'm waiting for Santoni."

Santoni drove up to the Maldonado home in his black hearse. A young assistant sat in the passenger seat.

Gonzalo walked Santoni to the body.

"That's a shame," Santoni said. It was what he said for every corpse he encountered.

He took a half-dozen Polaroid photos of the body, then Gonzalo helped Santoni put the body of Elena Maldonado in a black body bag and put the bag onto a hardbacked stretcher, the Polaroid on top of the bag, and carry the stretcher out to the hearse.

In all of this, the assistant had not moved from his seat.

"What does your assistant do?" Gonzalo whispered to the undertaker.

"Him?" Santoni was surprised. "He doesn't do anything. He's my son."

A minute after Santoni pulled away from the Maldonado house, Gonzalo was on his way to La Cola.

CHAPTER ELEVEN

Okay. If they're up there, we have to do two things. First, make sure they don't get away. Second, catch them."

Gonzalo spoke to his three deputies slowly. He felt the urge to race up into the hill and catch the bad guys. That was a police officer's job and duty. That's what one trained for. But he knew his deputies felt the same. Who, then was going to stay at the end of the road, at the bottom of the hill, and make sure no one escaped?

"Hector," he said, then he paused a moment. He was about to give Hector the job of waiting, but he thought better of it. Hector was young and fast. Whether it was a car chase or a footrace, no one was a more likely candidate for being able to catch a suspect, not even Gonzalo. Besides, no one in the entire Puerto Rican police department was a better shot than Hector.

Hector straightened when he heard his name. He had no idea what his sheriff was thinking.

Gonzalo held up a finger and looked at Wilfrido Vargas. Even with an injured arm, there was no doubt Vargas was not a man who could be easily overpowered. Certainly, he had to go on the house-to-house search.

Anibal Gomez was left. Gonzalo looked at the small man and saw nothing more than a small man; unable to stop anyone from escaping if it came to that.

"Hector, you take Anibal and go up to the top."

"Doña Sepulveda's house?"

"Her son's house," Gonzalo corrected, since Doña Sepulveda had been dead for three years.

"You two start from the top. Vargas, you head to Don Raul's house. Hector, you move your way down; Vargas, you head your way up. Between the two of you, knock on every door where people live and search every abandoned house."

"Even if it's covered with weeds?" Anibal interposed.

"Even if it's buried with weeds. I'll be here by the radio. If anyone starts to run, give me a call. Any questions?"

"What if they run into the woods? Do we call you or chase them?" Anibal asked.

"That's up to Hector. He'll make the decision if needed. Just do what he says."

The three officers drove off in their two separate cars. Gonzalo sat in the driver's seat of his car with the door open and one foot on the ground. The heat of the day was finally beginning to die away, but he did not yet feel cool. He played over and again in his mind what he would do if the chase brought the suspects to him. He checked to see if his gun was readily available to his quick reach.

The first door Officer Vargas knocked on belonged to Don Raul. Don Raul had moved up into the area of La Cola in the forties and was one of the first settlers. He had moved in alone and had stayed alone for nearly half a century and he wanted nothing more than to be alone for the rest of his days. Not many in Angustias had any interest in interfering with his plans.

The house seemed dark and abandoned.

"Don Raul!" Vargas yelled out.

"I don't want visitors!" Don Raul yelled back.

"This is Deputy Vargas. From the police. I need to talk to you."

"Did they steal my fence again?"

Officer Vargas had no idea what to say to this, but he wanted to say something that would keep Don Raul talking.

"Maybe!" he yelled in through a window.

Don Raul was lying on his sofa. His arm rested across his brow. His eyes were closed. After a minute, he got up and walked to the door.

"What do you want?"

"Have you seen a man who looked like Clemente up here in La Cola?"

"Who's Clemente?"

Since Roberto Clemente had been the most famous sports star in Puerto Rico's history, Vargas was amazed by the question.

"Baseball player . . . Tall, thin, dark, short hair. He's got a brother. Shorter, also dark, short hair."

"Go to the top of the hill, on the road just a little below Doña Sepulveda's. You can see them from here. Every few nights, they drive off the hill. Did they really take the fence?"

"No, I don't think they're the ones you want. I want them for something else."

"Did anyone take my fence?" Don Raul asked through the door.

Vargas looked around.

"Where was the fence?"

"In front of the house! Where would you put a fence?"

"Uh, there's no fence out here. . . . I think it was—"

"Are you going to help me?"

Vargas started to walk away.

"I'll be back. First I have to talk to the guy who looks like Clemente."

"You won't be back," Don Raul muttered to himself, making his way back to his sofa.

Hector and Anibal had not yet made it all the way up the twists and turns of the hill when Deputy

Vargas radioed them. He gave them directions, was told by Gonzalo to move to a position where he could monitor their approach to the house, and watched them until they made a turn that took them out of sight and brought them near the property they were searching for.

Hector Pareda and Anibal Gomez approached the location given to them. The house was an unpainted wooden structure standing a foot off the ground, supported by a dozen or so wooden posts in various stages of decay. The metal roof had rusted through in some places and was patched with flattened cracker cans. The plywood that made up the walls was bubbling and peeling in places. In front of the house, the grass had clearly not been cut since . . . since God himself had planted it. A dented and dirty blue Toyota sat on the grass, the weeds and shrubbery around it made it seem as though it had decided to nest there.

The area around was desolate. This was one of the nether reaches of the neighborhood. Any pretense at road maintenance had stopped ten years earlier, so that Hector had to slowly drive into and out of a number of potholes large enough to park the car in. What was left of the road was so narrow that tall grass leaned over and touched the squad car on both sides. A mango tree some forty feet high spread its branches across the path and in another week or two it would drop its harvest by the bushel onto the ground below and feed a thousand flies.

As they got closer, the officers could hear arguing going on inside the house, but they couldn't tell what the argument was about. The loudest word was "*Idiota*," and it sounded like only one person was yelling.

"What do we arrest them for?" Anibal asked.

"What do you mean?" Hector whispered. "We arrest them because Gonzalo said so."

"No. I mean what's the charge?"

Hector sighed.

"Gonzalo wants to speak to them in connection with the murder of Elena Maldonado. We don't know more than that, and we don't need to know. Gonzalo will charge them when he wants with what he wants. All we do is make sure we bring them in."

"But . . ."

"Look. If you want, stay in the car; I'll bring them in."

Anibal pursed his lips, and Hector knew he could count on the deputy to do the job.

In the last ten yards or so before turning into the grassy area in front of the shack, the deputies noticed an abrupt end to the shouting. Hector parked at an angle behind the Toyota so that anyone trying to get away in that car would have to either push the squad car out of the way, drive through the house or detour through the underbrush.

As the deputies got out of the car, a man came to the door of the house, barefoot, and stared at them.

He had on jeans cut off at mid-calf and an orange T-shirt. There was a bandana tied about his head, and even from five yards away it was plain one of his eyes was swollen shut. He yelled something to the person inside and started running around to the back of the house.

"I'll get him!" Hector yelled, sprinting. "Get the other guy!"

Anibal ran to the house and caught a fist with his right temple as he stepped into the doorway. His head hit the doorpost, and his attacker tried to push his way out. However little Anibal may have appeared, he was not one to be pushed aside easily. Though he couldn't see his attacker, though the attacker was nearly a half-foot taller than him, he grabbed on to the man's belt with one hand as he passed and did not let go.

The man, Carlos Tejada, as they would find out later, tried to drag Anibal to the car, but soon tired of dragging the very live weight and felt his pants coming down. He decided instead to fight the small deputy.

Anibal could by no stretch of the imagination be called muscular. He was scrawny and nothing he had ever tried had been able to change that. But this did not stop him from finding that the middle of a fight was his natural element. While in every other situation his stature and thinness helped to make his moves seem awkward, in a fight he attained elegance.

Carlos swung for Anibal's head. Anibal ducked under the arm and landed a punch an inch or two above the waist that made Carlos hop. Carlos threw another punch, hitting nothing. Anibal stepped in and landed a punch at the bottom of his victim's sternum. For a second or maybe less, Carlos seemed unaffected by the punch; he straightened himself and brought his hands back to defend against another punch or prepare to throw another. At the end of that second, Carlos realized he had no air left in him and that his lungs had stopped trying to take any more in.

He threw another punch. Anibal ducked under it and landed another punch without straightening first. He hit Carlos at a point just above the genitals, and the man crumpled to the ground. Anibal approached him with some caution. Carlos had his mouth wide open as though crying hysterically though silently, and his face was nearly red, though he was normally brown-skinned.

"Do you need help breathing?" Anibal asked.

Carlos wouldn't have understood the question even if he could have focused on something outside of his private world of pain. Anibal took his silence for an affirmative response.

He brought his fist down with all his strength on the man's chest and Carlos gasped in. That final punch had hurt no less than any of the others Anibal had administered, but Carlos was grateful for it.

Anibal dragged his prisoner a few feet, moving him close to the back of the squad car, resting his head against a rear tire.

"It's your solar plexus," he said by way of explanation.

He stretched out Carlos's right arm, put a handcuff on the wrist and attached the other end to his left ankle.

"Don't move," he warned Carlos, "You'll only hurt yourself," but Carlos had no intention of going anywhere.

Anibal ran towards the back of the little house and was momentarily frozen by what he saw there. Behind the shack there was nothing. The hill simply ended. It was a terrain that might have been described as *barranco*, a steep decline. Maybe that was too guarded a term. Behind the house there was an almost sheer cliff. Not quite a 90 degree drop, but something close.

Hector was standing a few yards down the hillside no more than ten feet away from the second suspect. He stood in the middle of a bush that grew out of the side of the hill; with his left hand extended above his head, he held on to the trunk of a sapling.

His would-be prisoner, Pedro Tejada as they later found out, was in no better position. His left foot was buried at the root of a clump of tall grass. His left hand, also extended above his head, was clutching a small rock outcropping. With his right foot he was trying to kick out a foothold for his next step.

With enough time, and since Hector was going nowhere time was in abundance, he would carve a foothold out of the red clay dirt and be able to get another step away from his pursuer. There he could dig out another foothold and so on until he reached flatter land and the forest a dozen yards away. Clearly, this is where he was headed when he slipped partway down the mountainside. Hector had plunged after him impulsively. Below them both there was nothing for a hundred feet or more but a few more clumps of grass, scattered bushes, an occasional sapling, and, towards the end of a long slide, a thousand rocks and boulders.

Anibal watched the slow-motion chase for a moment, then ran back to his car. He came back a minute later, both men in the same position, both silently clinging to the mountainside. He threw a yellow, nylon utility rope down to Hector.

"Take the rope!" he yelled to his partner.

"What's it tied to?" Hector yelled back without having touched the cord.

"The tow knob on the car!" was the response.

Hector took hold of the rope, used it to swing over to Pedro Tejada. He tied Pedro's left leg and pumped his arm in the air, signaling that he was ready to be pulled off the hill.

Anibal ran back to the car, put it in reverse and eased the men off the cliffside. Pedro was not finished fighting. Though he was tied by a leg, though he was bruised, he jumped to his feet and swung at

Hector. The punch smashed into the officer's left temple, and Hector staggered back, almost falling off the cliffside. He straightened and headed for his prisoner again. Pedro repeated his first punch, landing it exactly as before. Hector fell in a heap, and Pedro knelt to untangle his leg from the rope. He stood again and turned and caught Anibal's fist directly between his eyes. With his hands dangling at his sides, he fell to his knees. He was falling forward when Anibal hit him with an uppercut to the bridge of his nose. Pedro collapsed. Anibal went to Hector's side.

"Are you okay?" he asked.

Hector sat a moment with his eyes closed. He moved his hand about his face as though trying to clear away a spider's web or make sure his face was still in its usual place.

"Are you okay?"

"Where are you?"

"Open your eyes."

"They're closed?"

"Here. Let me get your handcuffs. Rest a minute."

Anibal moved to cuff Pedro Tejada, but Pedro was just conscious enough to wriggle his arms loose from the officer's hold.

Anibal took his standard-issue mace canister from his gun belt and squirted Pedro from about a foot away.

"Don't make me use more of this stuff," he told his prisoner. "It gives me a headache."

Pedro was no further trouble to Anibal and allowed himself to be led stumbling to the squad car. He took a seat next to his brother.

"*No digas nada,*" he repeated over and over. "Don't say anything." His tone ranged from plea to advice to command to threat.

His brother said nothing in return and only looked out the car window, concentrating, as though still trying to figure out how he had wound up in the backseat of a police car in Angustias.

Hector was still a little dizzy from the punches he had received so he let Anibal do the driving back into town. He tried to start a conversation that might make the prisoners loosen their lips.

"Did you watch the Yankees last night?" Hector asked.

"I don't watch baseball," Anibal replied. When he looked at Hector, he understood he was supposed to play along.

"Why? What happened?" he asked.

"They lost again. Two on, no outs, and they couldn't push anyone across the plate."

"That's terrible," was all Anibal could think to say.

Hector was trying to work out a strategy where he could get the prisoners to say something, anything, but his partner was no help in this area. Pedro was the only one who had anything to say, and it wasn't very helpful.

"*No te voy decir nada.*" "I'm not going to tell you anything."

CHAPTER TWELVE

Gonzalo followed his three deputies into town. They all drove at a leisurely pace, as though there was nothing peculiar about the two men in handcuffs. As though the two men were under arrest for nothing worse than talking back to an officer or stealing a goat.

When they arrived in town, no one took any special notice of them. They parked in front of the precinct, and Gonzalo stepped around to lead the prisoners out of the car. Hector and Anibal headed into the station house.

"Get Marrero ready to move," Gonzalo called after them.

Hector nodded and went in.

Deputy Vargas led Carlos Tejada into the precinct, and Gonzalo was leading his taller brother in, holding him by the left elbow. As he reached the threshold, Pedro gave a jerk, pulled away from

Gonzalo, stooped over and dug his shoulder into Gonzalo's gut, knocking him over.

Gonzalo scrambled to his feet, but Pedro was already twenty feet away by then and headed for the town plaza. Gonzalo turned the corner just in time to see Pedro sprawl onto the plaza pavement as he tried to run past the bench where Don Justino sat. The old man had put out the crook of his cane to catch the handcuffed suspect. Pedro had jumped over the cane, never touching it. But he had twisted his ankle on landing and fallen hard.

Pedro struggled to push himself up to his feet again, but Don Justino rose from his bench and brought his cane down hard on the fugitive's hands, causing him to topple back to the ground in pain.

Don Justino held the cane over his head.

"*¡Quedate ai, criminal, si te quieres pa' algo!*" the old man yelled. "Stay there if you love yourself!"

Gonzalo came up quickly and jerked Pedro to his feet.

"Thanks for the help," he told Don Justino.

"Soon you're going to have to put me on the police force if you keep going like this," Don Justino responded as he took his seat again.

There were no more troubles in transporting the prisoner. Officer Vargas was given the task of moving Marrero out of the precinct temporarily. Marrero was moved to the offices of the mayor, where Vargas handcuffed him to a wooden chair and watched him. Marrero had nothing to say and promptly fell asleep.

At the station house, Gonzalo sat at his desk for a few minutes trying to figure out how best to conduct an interview of two suspects when the station house had no separate conference rooms. He prided himself on being able to trip up any suspect. He got a great number of confessions when prisoners got tired of trying to remember their lies. In fact, some habitual criminals have said over the years that they preferred being interrogated by Sheriff Molina in Comerio, a man who thought nothing of beating the truth out of a prisoner with a chair leg. At least Molina's questions didn't make them dizzy.

When he had formulated a strategy, he started.

"Hector, bring the short one over here."

Hector brought the shorter one to the sheriff, and Gonzalo got out of his chair.

"Sit," he told the prisoner.

Carlos looked to his brother before taking the seat. Pedro looked on with intense interest. He pursed his lips in anger.

"Did your brother tell you not to talk to me?" Gonzalo started.

"No," the young man lied.

"You don't have to talk to me. You understand that, right? It can't be held against you if you say nothing. You understand me?"

The young man looked to his brother.

"No digas na',*"* the brother said from his cell.

"That's good advice," Gonzalo said. "If you lie to me . . ."

"I'm not a liar," the younger brother said, hanging his head.

Gonzalo laughed.

"Of course not. Put him back in the cell."

Hector grabbed Carlos by the upper arm and pulled him out of the chair. He forced the young man into the cell roughly.

Gonzalo laughed again and spoke to Anibal in a familiar whisper just barely loud enough to excite interest in the brothers.

"What'd you say?" the younger brother asked.

"No seas intrometi'o. I'm not talking to you," Gonzalo answered.

"You're talking about me."

"Look. You killed a woman. You stabbed her seven times. You don't want to talk about it. I wouldn't want to talk about it either. Hector, bring the other one."

"I didn't do it!"

Hector and Gonzalo ignored the younger brother. When the older brother was in his seat, Gonzalo started again.

"Are you afraid to give your name too?"

The older brother was silent and looked away from the sheriff. Gonzalo took another chair and sat right in front of the suspect. He reached out and took a firm hold of the man's chin and turned the face back to face him.

"Look at me when I'm talking to you. You understand me?"

The young man looked at the sheriff and if his eyes could have gone out and killed him, Gonzalo would have been a dead man.

"Good. Now I'm trying to figure out who is the stupid one of you two. I've got good news and bad news for you guys. You want to hear me?"

The suspect sat quietly in his chair. He knew Gonzalo wanted to tell him something and would say it without being asked.

"Well, we might drop the charges about the assault on the old man. That's the good news."

The suspect still had nothing to say.

"Do you want to hear the bad news? No? Well, then I won't explain much, just the basics. There was evidence left behind. A week or two from now, when we go to the grand jury, we will say it was left during the murder. If anyone says, 'No. Wait a minute. That evidence was left during a break-in, during the assault on the old man.' The judge will look to me, and I will shrug my shoulders and say, 'I don't have a record of this phantom assault.' Whose fingerprints will I find on this evidence?"

The young man set his jaw more firmly. His brother approached the bars of his cell.

"What kind of evidence did you find?"

Gonzalo continued staring at the man in front of him.

"What kind of evidence?"

"Put him back in his cell," Gonzalo said getting to his feet.

"What kind of evidence?" the younger brother insisted. "Answer me!"

Hector locked away the older brother as Gonzalo walked out of the precinct.

"Answer me!" the younger brother yelled again.

"Stop screaming," Hector ordered. "He's not going to answer your questions."

"Why not?" The brother was distraught.

"This is his precinct. He asks the questions here. He doesn't answer them. That's your job."

Hector made the cell door secure and followed his sheriff outside. Gonzalo was sitting on the step in front of the station house door, and Hector sat beside him. Hector looked around before talking and even though there was no one within hearing range, he spoke softly.

"Did we find evidence in the Maldonado home?"

"We did now. If they think it's there, it has to be there, don't you think?"

Anibal stepped out of the station house to join them.

"The tall one says he wants a lawyer."

"You left them alone in there?" Gonzalo asked.

"He says he wants a lawyer. I thought you should know."

156

"Don't leave murderers alone unless it's an emergency."

Anibal blinked, trying to think.

"Like what kind of emergency?"

"Like you're dead already. Get back in there."

Anibal left Hector and the sheriff, closing the door gently as he reentered the station house.

"Do you have the evidence kit in the car?" Gonzalo asked.

"You want me to go to the Maldonado house?"

"I want you to go to that car, the Toyota. Lift prints, take pictures, pop the trunk, look in the glove compartment. I'll get Nuñez to get us a warrant for all this. I'll radio you when we have it. I'm going to run the plate numbers; if it comes back stolen we don't even need the warrant. The house is open, right?"

"Yeah."

"Well, since we know it's a crime scene, you can start looking there."

"What crime?" Hector asked.

Gonzalo's eyes grew wide. For a moment he was speechless.

"What do you mean, 'What crime'? You were attacked there; Anibal was punched in the head as soon as he got in the door. That house is a crime scene, Hector. Now go. I'll radio you about opening the car."

Hector started to his squad car, but paused when Wilfrido Vargas rounded the corner.

"How's the prisoner?" Gonzalo asked.

"Sleeping like a baby. Nuñez had me cuff him to a chair in his office. He keeps a gun locked in his desk. Does he know how to use it?"

"Learn this about Jorge Nuñez—the deputy mayor is a very serious man and wouldn't have a gun if he didn't know how to use it," Gonzalo replied very solemnly.

"Well, I don't think he'll need it anytime soon. Marrero couldn't get out of his chair even without the handcuffs. In fact, I had to help him get into the chair."

"Well, I think this investigation is beginning to wind down. Take a turn around the town. Go to Colmado Ruiz, let yourself be seen. Visit Iris at the Maldonado place for a few minutes. Report back here in, let me see, forty-five minutes."

"Can I get something to eat?"

"Sure. Didn't you get anything when I told you to? Go to Cafetin Lolita if you want."

"I'll get something at Colmado Ruiz."

"Whatever you want . . . Just remind the people of Angustias that there is a police presence."

"What are you going to be doing, chief?" Hector asked as he slipped into the driver's seat.

"I've got phone calls to make."

Hector pulled away.

"I guess I'll be headed out too," Vargas said and he turned to get into his own car.

"Wait a minute," Gonzalo said, and he dug into

his pocket and brought out a small bunch of folded singles.

"I need you to do me a favor."

He gave his deputy the money and instructions.

"Go over to the supermarket here and get formula for an infant, two days old; Lucinda will tell you what to get. Take it to my wife. Tell her I'll be over later with clothes for the baby."

Vargas did as he was told and was accosted in the supermarket by Lucinda, the store owner's wife, and a small group of shoppers.

"What happened?"

"I don't know anything. All I need is a can of milk for a baby—two days old."

"You want two-day-old milk for a baby?" asked one lady.

"The baby is two days old. . . ."

"I see . . . Is someone dead?"

"I can't tell you."

"Don't you know what a dead person looks like? Don't they show you in the police academy?" asked Don Feliciano, who was sitting on a pile of rice sacks.

"I've seen dead people before. I just can't say whether anyone is dead. . . ."

"Of course someone is dead," Doña Lucinda spoke up. "A mother, a new mother. There's only one new mother in Angustias. . . ."

"Who said it was a mother?" Vargas asked as he

accepted the can of formula from Doña Lucinda behind the counter.

"What do you think I am, stupid? I don't think you're having trouble breast-feeding. Elena Maldonado is dead. She's the only new mother in town. Am I right or wrong?"

Officer Vargas tossed two dollars onto the counter for the $1.99 can and left without saying another word.

"*Ese no sabe na'*," he heard as he left the store. "That one doesn't know anything."

As he drove to Gonzalo's house to make the delivery, he tried to inventory what it was that he did know about the case. Aside from what Doña Lucinda had already figured out for herself, he knew little, and he wondered whether he was being kept in the dark intentionally.

At Gonzalo's house, Mari opened the door as soon as he had shut off the engine. The baby was asleep in her arms. Mari waved Vargas into the house.

"Speak softly," she warned him before he had said a word.

"Gonzalo just told me to bring you this." He handed her the can of formula. "He said he would bring clothes a little later."

"Have they brought in the guy who beat up Collazo?"

"Two guys. They look like brothers."

"Did my husband interrogate them yet?"

"I'm not sure. I think so. I think we're looking at them as the murderers of Elena."

"It wasn't Marcos?"

Vargas shrugged, turning the palms of his hands upwards.

"Gonzalo hasn't told you much?"

"I don't think he's told anybody much. . . . He has a lot of running around to do."

"Wow, that means he hasn't had time to think things out. He talks to himself when he's putting the puzzle together. If not, he'll talk to whoever's around him. He asks questions when he feels close. If you give him the answer he has in mind, he thinks he's right. . . ."

"What if I give the wrong answer?" Vargas wanted to know.

"Do what Collazo used to do . . . Just say, 'I dunno.'"

Vargas laughed out loud at the face Mari put on to emulate Collazo, and the baby began to stir when he heard the sound. Mari shooed the officer away.

"Go away before the baby wakes up. Remind Gonzalo about the baby clothes."

The child started to cry as soon as the door closed behind him, and Vargas was glad to be out of the house. He made Colmado Ruiz his first stop in making the rounds of Angustias. There he found Ruiz using the stub of his right arm to pass an almost clean rag across the counter.

"How can I help you, Officer?"

Though Vargas had only been on the force in Angustias for a few weeks, he knew already that Ruiz only addressed officers as "officer" when he was nervous or had had a drink or two.

"I just need a couple of sodas, one Coke, one Pepsi. You got any hot bread?"

"I can heat some."

"Give me a pound with butter."

While Ruiz went to heat the bread in a small convection oven that served only to heat bread and coffee, Vargas leaned over the counter to peek into the garbage can. There were two bottles of beer with the sweat still on them.

"Have you been drinking?"

"*Ay, caramba!*" Ruiz responded.

"What?"

"I burned myself with the tray." Ruiz slammed the heated bread onto the counter and buttered it savagely as though trying to make it pay for the burn he had suffered.

"Ruiz . . . Look at me. . . . Have you been drinking?"

"I'm old enough to drink if I want to."

"But it's only five o'clock. . . . You're supposed to be running the store."

"Look. Officer, it's been a bad day, okay?"

"Okay. Sure. But if I find you drunk in public, your day is going to get worse."

Vargas paid three dollars for his sodas and bread and was about to leave.

"One thing, Officer . . . Perfecto is dead, right?"

"Perfecto is dead," Vargas answered, and he noticed Ruiz exhale with relief.

"Why do you want to know?"

"No reason. No reason. He owed me money."

"Was it a lot?"

"What difference does it make if he's dead?"

Officer Vargas couldn't think of anything to overcome that argument, so he turned and left the store. His next stop was the Maldonado home. Officer Calderon was standing on the porch and waved to him as he parked.

"I brought you a soda and some bread," he called out.

"You're a lifesaver. I thought I was going to grow old and die here before anyone remembered to get me anything."

"Any trouble here?"

"Nope."

"Any news?"

Iris Calderon was chewing away at a piece of buttered bread she hadn't even taken completely out of the brown bag yet.

"They took the body away, thank God. Also, Gonzalo doesn't think it was Marcos."

"What do you mean? Why not?"

"No real reason . . . I mean, nothing you can take

163

to court, yet. The knife doesn't match any of the sets they have here. He took a beer bottle that might have the fingerprints of a third party. . . ."

"The guy who killed Elena?"

"Maybe."

"Is Marcos no longer our main suspect for the murder?"

"I think another hour or two should tell."

Calderon kept eating. Though she was perennially thin and no one had ever seen or heard her to struggle to maintain her weight, she could eat about as much Vargas, who likely doubled her weight.

"What about the guy who beat up Collazo? Any idea where he fits in?"

"Another hour or two should tell us that too, I guess."

"Don't we know anything for sure yet?"

"The case is turning out to be a little more complicated than we first thought it was when we brought Marcos in. I think this is pretty natural. Solving a murder isn't supposed to be like watching *Columbo* on TV. We don't get to see who the murderer is, then put the evidence together. For us, it's the other way around."

Vargas was silent a moment. Throughout the conversation he had hardly taken a bite of his bread or a sip of his soda. Calderon could tell there was something on his mind. He raised the bottle to his lips.

"Does that hurt?" she asked, pointing to the bandage that covered the stitches on his forearm.

"Not as much as it did Maldonado."

"Yeah, well I figure that guy abused his wife the last few years, and he's not dead yet, so he hasn't gotten what he deserves. Yet."

Vargas nodded.

"I guess you're right, but wouldn't it be funny?"

"What?"

"I mean if Marcos Maldonado is the only innocent person, and he got attacked like that."

"Hilarious," Calderon replied, and she finished her buttered bread and her soda.

GET UP TO 4 FREE BOOKS!

You can have the best fiction delivered to your door for less than what you'd pay in a bookstore or online—only $4.25 a book! Sign up for our book clubs today, and we'll send you **FREE* BOOKS** just for trying it out...**with no obligation to buy, ever!**

LEISURE HORROR BOOK CLUB

With more award-winning horror authors than any other publisher, it's easy to see why CNN.com says "Leisure Books has been leading the way in paperback horror novels." Your shipments will include authors such as RICHARD LAYMON, DOUGLAS CLEGG, JACK KETCHUM, MARY ANN MITCHELL, and many more.

LEISURE THRILLER BOOK CLUB

If you love fast-paced page-turners, you won't want to miss any of the books in Leisure's thriller line. Filled with gripping tension and edge-of-your-seat excitement, these titles feature everything from psychological suspense to legal thrillers to police procedurals and more!

As a book club member you also receive the following special benefits:
- **30% OFF all orders through our website & telecenter!**
- **Exclusive access to special discounts!**
- **Convenient home delivery and 10 days to return any books you don't want to keep.**

There is no minimum number of books to buy, and you may cancel membership at any time. See back to sign up!

*Please include $2.00 for shipping and handling.

YES! ☐

Sign me up for the Leisure Horror Book Club and send my TWO FREE BOOKS! If I choose to stay in the club, I will pay only $8.50* each month, a savings of $5.48!

YES! ☐

Sign me up for the Leisure Thriller Book Club and send my TWO FREE BOOKS! If I choose to stay in the club, I will pay only $8.50* each month, a savings of $5.48!

NAME: _____

ADDRESS: _____

_____

TELEPHONE: _____

E-MAIL: _____

☐ **I WANT TO PAY BY CREDIT CARD.**

☐ VISA   ☐ MasterCard.   ☐ DISCOVER

ACCOUNT #: _____

EXPIRATION DATE: _____

SIGNATURE: _____

Send this card along with $2.00 shipping & handling for each club you wish to join, to:

Horror/Thriller Book Clubs
1 Mechanic Street
Norwalk, CT 06850-3431

Or fax (must include credit card information!) to: 610.995.9274. You can also sign up online at www.dorchesterpub.com.

*Plus $2.00 for shipping. Offer open to residents of the U.S. and Canada only. Canadian residents please call 1.800.481.9191 for pricing information.

If under 18, a parent or guardian must sign. Terms, prices and conditions subject to change. Subscription subject to acceptance. Dorchester Publishing reserves the right to reject any order or cancel any subscription.

JOIN NOW!

CHAPTER THIRTEEN

"Officer Estrada, where are you?" Gonzalo spoke into his radio.

"I'm at the elementary school. . . ."

"What are you doing there?"

"One of the teachers has a blue Toyota parked here. I was checking it out. Then a fight broke out—three sixth-graders against two fourth-graders."

"Did you use your nightstick or your gun?"

"Both."

"I've got a trip for you . . . Santurce. You'll be meeting a friend of mine at the precinct there. I've given him the information on some guys we have here. He'll take you around to talk to some people who might know something about this case."

Gonzalo gave his deputy some directions and the name of the sergeant he would be meeting with. Being happy to have something useful to do, Estrada didn't ask many questions. He took down the names of the sixth-graders, scaring them thoroughly, and drove off for Santurce.

At Gonzalo's end of the investigation, the plate numbers on the Toyota came back as being registered to another Toyota that was still parked in front of a home in Santurce. Only the front plate had been taken, and the owner had no idea when that had happened. All this, Gonzalo was able to learn from two five-minute phone calls, one to run the plates and the other to the owner.

In a third phone call, he spoke to a friend in the metropolitan police to confirm that a blue Toyota had been reported stolen in the past few weeks.

"I've got records for about a dozen blue Toyotas. It's their most popular color. Do you have a serial number?"

"Not yet. Listen. Any of the cars taken from Santurce?"

There was a slight shuffle of papers and a long "ummmm."

"That narrows it down to three. Do you want the information on them?"

"Sure."

Gonzalo took information about the owners and where the cars were last seen. None of the three from Santurce had been taken any more recently than a week before.

The phone rang as soon as he hung up. On the other end of the line the deputy mayor sounded more anxious than Gonzalo had ever heard him.

Jorge Nuñez was the antithesis of Mayor Ramirez, who was high-strung and bossy. Nuñez kept his calm in all situations.

"You have to get over here."

"What's wrong? Is Marrero giving you trouble?"

"Just get over here," Nuñez snapped and hung up.

Gonzalo put the receiver down on his end and thought about his situation a few seconds before getting up to leave. He had more officers at his command than he had had through the first decade of his time as the sheriff of Angustias, but the crimes he had tackled in recent years seemed to stretch his forces to their limits. This particular crime was beginning to wear on him though it was only a few hours old.

"Don't let them talk to each other," he ordered Anibal. "And don't leave them alone even for a second."

"When do I get my phone call?" Pedro asked, but Gonzalo ignored him and left the precinct.

The station house was attached to the back end of the *alcaldia*, sticking out of the ancient building something like a wart. Gonzalo walked around to the front door of the government building; Nuñez was waiting for him there.

"What's the matter? Is Marrero causing—"

"Get in, get in."

Gonzalo obliged the deputy mayor. Nuñez turned to the sheriff in the lobby.

"He says he was fighting a guy in Colmado Ruiz."

"That's why he's under arrest."

"Yes, fine, but he says the guy he was fighting was Elena Maldonado's boyfriend. He says that if Elena's dead then this guy probably did it. What do we say, Gonzalo?"

Gonzalo didn't know what to say. The picture wasn't just murkier, it was more dangerous. If a killer was still on the loose, Hector could be walking into a trap. Iris Calderon could be the target of an attack. If there was a third person involved in the murder of Elena Maldonado, who knew how many other people might be joined in one way or another to this conspiracy.

"Is he still talking?"

"He fell asleep again."

"I'll be back in a couple of minutes. I need to get to a radio."

Gonzalo left the building before Nuñez could remind him that the mayor's office had a radio.

From his car, the sheriff radioed Officer Calderon.

"There might be another guy to look out for. A third assassin. Keep your eyes open."

"What does he look like?"

"You know better than I. Marrero says the guy he was fighting with in Colmado Ruiz was Elena's boyfriend."

"Wow."

"Yeah, wow. Just keep your gun ready and don't hesitate if he comes to the house."

"Got it."

Next, Gonzalo got on the radio to contact Hector, but there was no immediate response, and the sheriff started up his car. Before he had gotten very far from the center of Angustias, Hector radioed him back.

"Can you give me a minute?" he said.

Hector's voice told Gonzalo that his young deputy was concentrating and in the brief time the channel had been open he could hear a car engine running.

"What are you doing?" Gonzalo asked back, but there was no response at all this time except for another second of open channel and running engine noise.

"Is everything under control?" he asked,

"Give me a minute," Hector repeated, annoyance lacing his voice.

Gonzalo pulled his car over to the side of the road, put the car in park, and sat behind the wheel with the CB mike in his hand, resting in his lap.

In his car, Hector had flung the mike on the passenger seat. He had arrived at La Cola only a few minutes before to find that the blue Toyota was gone. He knew he hadn't passed it on the way up the mountain, and the road was too narrow for two cars. Still, there were more than a dozen driveways and partially completed driveways that branched off the road. Most were abandoned to be overrun

171

by weeds that tried to reclaim the pavement for the forest. Hector was trying to get off the hill as fast as he could, while still peering into every opening in the woods that could hold a car. Then he caught a glimpse of the car through a break in the foliage.

It was slowly backing out of a narrow dead-end entrance near the bottom of the hill.

"Hector, I need you to come in," Gonzalo insisted over the CB.

Trying to keep his eyes on the curves of the road and on the spot where the blue Toyota should be if the foliage allowed him to see clearly, Hector used one hand to fish for the mike he had thrown aside.

"I'm following the Toyota out of El Culo, and it looks like it's headed south, I think, on Route One-one-seven. I'll keep you posted. Out."

His *out* was emphatic, and Gonzalo knew it would be best to wait for a report without bothering Hector as he drove. Hector was a capable officer; he knew what he was doing. These thoughts were enough to keep Gonzalo off the CB, but they did nothing to stop him from driving toward La Cola. After all, if the blue car wasn't headed south, if it was headed north, it was headed right for him.

Sure enough, the blue Toyota and Hector's squad car were pulled over onto the side of the road facing north when Gonzalo came upon them a few minutes later. Hector was approaching the driver's side of the car. His right hand rested on his holstered sidearm.

Gonzalo slowed a few yards before reaching the parked cars and made a U-turn, pulling up close in front of the Toyota and reversing to get in even closer. He looked at the driver through his rearview mirror and could see he was nervous. He didn't like this at all. Nervous suspects did stupid things—they ran, they struggled, they reached for weapons.

"License and registration, sir," was all Hector said when he got to the driver's window. He stretched out his left hand, waiting for the papers.

"Is there something wrong, Officer?"

"You're not giving me the documentation I need. Without those papers, I need to take you to the station house," Hector said evenly. Gonzalo admired what he heard; his deputy made it seem like nothing more was wrong than a forgivable poor lane change or an almost negligible case of speeding.

The driver fumbled for his papers, and Hector walked back to his squad car calmly once he had them in hand. He ducked his head into the car, resting his elbows on the car door windowsill. After a moment, he headed back to the Toyota.

"I need you to step out of the car," he said, and he opened the door for the suspect.

The driver was a small man, smaller than Hector at least. He had dark skin and hair cut close to the scalp. His nose looked like it had been hit with a pool cue—

though hours had passed since the incident in Colmado Ruiz the ridge of the nose still bled somewhat. There was swelling, and this swelling was beginning to spread to the area under the eyes. Gonzalo had seen enough barroom brawlers to know that the injured face would get uglier before getting better.

The man shrugged as he stepped onto the shoulder of the road.

"What's wrong? I did nothing," he protested.

"The license plate number on the registration doesn't match the one on the car. I need you to come with me."

Gonzalo watched in his side-view mirror as Hector put a hand on the driver's arm. The driver pulled away and seemed to want to climb back into his car, but Hector gave the man a sharp kick at the back of his right knee and with his hand on the man's chest, the deputy slammed him into the pavement.

The man put his hands up in front of his face as though he expected to be attacked. Hector put a handcuff on one wrist, flipped the driver onto his belly and cuffed his other wrist. This was the work of a second, and Hector had the prisoner on his feet by the time Gonzalo got to his side. The sheriff reminded himself that when he meant to spring into action in the future, he had better actually spring.

"Need any help?" he asked though it was clear the situation was under control.

"Do you want to take him in while I work on the car?"

Gonzalo thought for a second.

"I've got to speak to Marcos. Get Vargas to transport the prisoner. . . ."

"Where to?"

The station house in Angustias was full and this prisoner clearly couldn't be put in the *alcaldia* with Marrero, the man who had smashed his nose.

"Take him to the church," Gonzalo decided.

"I think it's too late for him, boss," Hector said, and he was serious.

"Not for confession, Hector. They have a few offices that they don't use. Have Vargas sit in one of them with him until I'm ready to move him."

"The priest won't mind?"

"He might, but we don't have too many options. Tell Vargas that if he has any trouble, he can have Father Moreno call me at the precinct."

"But are you going to be in?"

Gonzalo shrugged as he walked back to his car.

"I'm going to the clinic for a few minutes. I'll see where I go from there."

Gonzalo drove off towards the clinic, and Hector shook his head as he walked back to his car. He had faced many busy days as a deputy in Angustias, but they had never resorted to placing a suspect in the church. He knew there would be a service within the hour—sparsely attended since it wasn't Sunday, but there'd be women and children in the same building with a man who might be a murderer. The way he saw it, the problem wouldn't be trying to convince Father Moreno to agree to warehouse the prisoner, it would be in trying to keep Father Moreno from exploding when he heard the plan.

Luckily for Officer Vargas, Father Moreno was listening to the confessions of Petra Betances when he brought the suspect into the church. Vargas walked his man up the center aisle of the church, stopping to genuflect with his prisoner before the altar as he headed towards the back of the church where the offices were.

Father Moreno watched from the confession booth, as the two men walked through his church, and he could make out the handcuffs that kept the prisoner's arms pinned behind his back. Still, there was nothing he could do to stop the deputy. Petra Betances was a sinful woman—she had always been sinful, would probably always be sinful, and seemed to take a special pleasure in telling her priest all about her wicked ways. When he saw Vargas, Father Moreno tried to get Petra to hurry through's her catalogue of misdeeds.

"Is the next sin like that last one? The same type?"

"Well . . ." Petra thought for a moment. She was no theologian. "Well, yes. But this one was married . . ."

"That's his sin, my child. For you it's the same."

"Should I say Hail Marys for this one too?"

"Do you have any other sins today? Something of a different type? Anger maybe? Or greed?"

Petra thought again, but could come up with nothing new.

"Then, my child, I want you to say the Hail Marys as I told you before, but I also want you to do one more thing."

"What is it father? I'd do anything to be rid of my sins. . . ."

For a moment, Father Moreno was certain he was being propositioned, but he put that thought aside.

"I want you to read the four gospels; Matthew, Mark, Luke, and John. We will discuss them next week; we'll set up an appointment. . . ."

"I don't own a Bible. . . . Father" Moreno could tell by her whispered voice that she was genuinely ashamed to admit this fact.

"Take one from the pews before you leave today."

"I can't . . ."

"With my blessing. Now go in peace." He absolved her and left the confessional before she had finished crossing herself.

"What is the meaning of this?" he demanded of Officer Vargas.

"Gonzalo's orders. We've run out of room for our prisoners. We need to hold him here for a—"

"Impossible. I cannot allow a criminal . . ."

"He's not convicted yet, Father. . . ."

"A possible criminal, then. I can't have a possible criminal here when the mass begins. . . ."

"I'll be with him one hundred percent of the time. . . ."

"That's not good enough. I don't want to be rude, but weren't you with Marcos Maldonado?"

Vargas straightened under the lash of this reminder and Father Moreno knew he had misspoken.

"I—"

"Gonzalo should be in the precinct by now, Father, if you'd like to speak with him. All I know is that I have orders to keep this guy here."

Father Moreno opened his mouth as if to say something, but decided against it. Instead, he went to his own office, prepared for that evening's mass, and did not bother with a phone call to the sheriff.

CHAPTER FOURTEEN

Gonzalo glanced at the dashboard clock through his steering wheel as he approached the clinic. It read 6:30.

Dr. Perez was standing in the parking lot of the clinic, leaning against a wall, smoking a cigarette. He waved to Gonzalo as he parked.

"Your prisoner is awake."

"Has he said anything?" Gonzalo didn't often find Dr. Perez in a talkative mood and wanted to exploit the fact that the doctor seemed open to conversation.

Dr. Perez shrugged.

"I don't think he's said anything that can help you."

"What did he say?"

"He says it wasn't him. I imagine most criminals say that."

"Anything else?"

"He asks how much morphine he can have. He's

not on morphine. He also wanted to know if he was going to get a sponge bath."

"Is he?" Gonzalo asked.

"I'll give him one before I leave tonight."

"I'm sure that's not what he meant."

Dr. Perez shrugged again.

"We don't always get what we want in life," he said.

"Marcos hasn't confessed or denied anything has he?"

Dr. Perez shook his head no. Gonzalo turned to enter the clinic, but turned again, remembering something.

"How's Marcos's health? Is he guaranteed to live?"

"He'll be fine. If the chop in the back had penetrated an inch deeper, he wouldn't have made it to the clinic. Two inches to the left and his spinal cord would have been severed. In a few weeks when the cast comes off his biggest worry will be that the shin will always tell him when it's about to rain." Dr. Perez took a last drag of his cigarette, dropped the cigarette butt, and squished it like a bug.

"It's pretty dry on this side of the island," the sheriff answered.

"It'll tell him when it's going to be dry too."

Inside the clinic, Marcos Maldonado had his right wrist handcuffed to the metal railing, an IV needle was dripping fluids into his arm. Pillows propped him most of the way onto his right side, and as the sheriff walked in through the door of the room, Marcos's butt was showing through his open-back gown.

"Cover yourself, Marcos," Gonzalo said as he did the job for his prisoner, covering him with the starched, white hospital sheet.

"How am I supposed to cover myself? I can't move my arms. The nurses don't help me."

"Why not?"

Marcos didn't want to say, and Gonzalo was left to guess that Marcos had said the wrong thing to the wrong nurse and had been left to fend for himself.

After covering Marcos, the sheriff pulled a chair to the side of his bed, sitting where it would be difficult for Marcos to escape looking straight at him without contorting himself painfully. After an awkward, silent moment, Marcos spoke first.

"Now that you're here, can you pass me the remote?"

"This is not a social visit, Marcos. You remember your Miranda rights? You don't have to talk with me without a lawyer unless you want to."

Marcos looked down at his shackled wrist and seemed to struggle to remember something.

"I didn't do it."

"Do what, Marcos?"

"I didn't do what you think I did."

"What do I think?"

"I didn't hurt Elena."

"That's hard to believe, Marcos. Do you know what happened to her?"

Marcos looked directly at Gonzalo and searched his face. Gonzalo knew what he was looking for.

Marcos wanted to know if the discussion was about murder or a simple assault. The sheriff arched an eyebrow, and Marcos read the worst from that.

"She's dead, right?"

"Yep. She's dead. Hector found you in the house with a knife in your hand, blood on your shirt. I think you may have gone a little too far this time. If we had the death penalty in Puerto Rico, you would fry."

"I didn't do it."

Gonzalo sighed, then chuckled to himself.

"You know, Marcos, I would believe you except for one thing. . . ."

"What?"

"Ninety-nine percent of men found with knives in their hands and blood on their shirts say the exact same thing. When you get to the penitentiary, you'll find out—everybody's innocent. Every victim stabbed themselves."

"No, it really wasn't me. There was a guy. He stabbed her. He stabbed me too. Look."

Marcos pointed to the cut on his arm. Gonzalo looked closely at the bandage.

"You want me to be impressed by that? If you want to help yourself, just tell me who did kill Elena. I'll be happy to knock on that person's door and bring them in."

Gonzalo waited for an answer. Marcos seemed to struggle with some inner conflict.

"I can't tell you. . . . But I didn't do it."

"Why can't you tell me, Marcos? You want me to give you my theory? I think you can't give me a name because there is no one to give me. You did it."

Gonzalo rose from his chair as part of a dramatic act intended to make Marcos feel that his moment to redeem himself had arrived and was slipping away. Marcos spoke.

"Elena had a boyfriend," he said.

Gonzalo tried to remain composed, hiding the fact that he never imagined that Marcos knew. Marcos was looking away, trying to bury his face in his pillow.

"How long have you known about this?"

"A month, maybe two months. I'm not positive. I've been drinking a lot."

"How did you find out about this?"

"People whisper—*A ese le estan pagando cuerno*— That guy's wife is cheating on him."

"Who told you directly?"

"Nobody told me directly. Would you tell someone something like that?"

"I might, depending on the person."

"Well, you're strange. Nobody told me. Not to my face. I just overheard a few things here and there; I put things together. I finished high school. I'm not stupid. I drove away one night. I told Elena I was going to Colmado Ruiz, you know, for a drink. . . ."

"One drink?"

"A few, whatever you want, it makes no difference. I drove up the hill, turned around, put the car in neutral, came down the hill, parked a few dozen yards away—you know where the *palo de pana* is? The one by the side of the road? I waited there. Ten minutes later, he came driving in."

"It's pretty dark in that area at night. Did you get a good look at him?"

"Short, dark skin, blue Toyota. Marrero said he's seen him before."

"He talked to you about this to your face?"

"I talked to him that night. I told him what I saw. He told me he knew about it for months. *Esa puta.* She got what she deserved."

"So what did you do about this?" Gonzalo asked.

"What did I do? What was I supposed to do? I can't hit a pregnant woman. By the time I knew about it, her belly was out to there."

Gonzalo was often amazed by the selective morality of his prisoners. This was one point he had heard before—it was all right to hit a woman, but not a pregnant one.

"So you did nothing?" he asked.

"I waited. I was going to give her a good beating today, but this guy was in there already when I woke up. I woke up because she screamed. I sat in the chair. She screamed again. I tried to get out of the chair, but this guy slashed my arm. I sat down again. I was falling asleep again when Hector came in."

"Falling asleep with a cut like that in your arm?"

"I had a few beers in me."

"A few?"

"Look. I didn't do it. Look for her boyfriend. Short, dark skin, owns a blue Toyota. If you show me a picture, I can pick him out." Marcos tried turning his face into his pillow again.

"I have one more question for you, Marcos, then I'll go. You say the boyfriend killed Elena?"

Marcos nodded.

"Do you have any idea why he killed her? Were they arguing about something?"

"How am I supposed to know? I just woke up in time to get slashed in the arm. . . ."

"Well, you can see how it can make a big difference, can't you?"

"To you maybe, not to me. You need a motive, but I don't know why he killed her—I don't care either. She got what she deserved, and when you catch him, he'll get what he deserves too."

"Let me remind you, Marcos. Your story right now doesn't work unless we can find that boyfriend. Even if we do, I can see it all happening this way—he came to the house and you killed her out of jealousy. Trying to defend her, the boyfriend slashes at you but when he sees she's dead, he runs out of the house. See, the boyfriend angle can work both ways."

Marcos had nothing to say to this, so Gonzalo left him, instructing Dr. Perez on his way out that Marcos should be considered dangerous.

"Don't try to take off his handcuffs. Don't let him have any visitors. One of my deputies will be here in a few minutes to sit with him."

"Did he really kill Elena?" Dr. Perez asked.

"I can't say at this time. I know this much—he's no angel."

Dr. Perez agreed to keep the other medical staff away from Marcos unless there was an emergency.

In the parking lot of the clinic, Gonzalo sat to think through all that he knew. He tried to separate the facts he had from the rumors and the actual connections between facts from the connections he had developed in his own imagination. After a minute, he decided he didn't really have much concrete to go on. He wanted to talk to all the other people he had in custody, but he refrained.

"I'd better get a few more facts," he told himself.

He drove off, taking a leisurely pace, reminding himself that he hadn't paid much attention to his wife and the Maldonado baby. He also hadn't heard from the Department of Child Welfare. He didn't want the child to stay in his house overnight—his wife would get overly attached and would be melancholy when the child was finally taken away. He wound up in front of his own home, though he had originally intended to go straight to the station house.

Mari was sitting in a rocking chair on the front porch, the baby in her arms. She rocked gently and patted his back. Gonzalo watched her from his car, and she paid no attention to him. He knew then that she had already grown fond of the boy and giving him up would be difficult for her.

"How's the baby?" Gonzalo tried to sound casual. Mari was a passionate woman who rarely brooked opposition once her mind was made up, and Gonzalo feared she might have already made up her mind to be a foster mother or perhaps even an adoptive mother to this child.

"Isn't he beautiful?" Mari answered, and Gonzalo knew there was trouble in the question. She was already trying to win him over to her way of seeing things.

"Is he sleeping?"

"He sleeps like an angel."

"You haven't heard anything from the child welfare people, have you?"

Mari was silent for a moment longer than Gonzalo would have liked.

"It would be a shame if the boy had to grow up with strangers, wouldn't it?"

"He won't."

"What do you mean? Does he have any relatives?"

"He might have some . . ."

"From whose side of the family? Both sides are worthless."

"Maybe not everybody is worthless, Mari. He might have some very nice relatives."

"But it would take a while to find them, to make sure they're good people. . . ."

"Not too long. . . ."

"At least a few days."

"Yeah, but the children's services department has a long list of homes that can care for him until—"

"Why can't we keep him until you find his good relatives?"

Gonzalo closed his eyes and meditated for a second, searching for a painless answer. He couldn't find one.

"We're not certified as foster parents. We're not related to the child. I don't think they would make any exceptions for us just because I'm a police officer."

"But we could try."

This was neither a plea nor a suggestion. Instead, Mari was dictating which course of action she would insist on, and Gonzalo could not think of any way of denying her, nor did he much want to when he looked at her cradling the infant. He knew they were both getting too old to care for an infant. He knew the government would not allow the child to stay with them. He knew the vision of Mari holding the child was a delusion, but he couldn't bring himself in that moment to refuse his wife the hope she held. He could not resist the power of the sight in front of him.

"We could try," Mari insisted, and Gonzalo nodded.

"Do you know who to call?" he asked, telling himself all the while that this was not the adoption of some abandoned dog that he was agreeing to.

"I spoke with them already," Mari said. "They're coming over to take the child, but I'll talk to them when they get here."

"So this was arranged before you even got a chance to speak with me?"

"Nothing's arranged. They're coming here to take the baby. Now that you told me it's okay to keep the baby, I have to talk to them, that's all."

Mari smiled at her husband, and he could not think of what to say in protest.

"Okay," he said, and he shrugged and walked back toward the car.

"When are you bringing the baby's clothes?" Mari shouted as he got in the car.

"I'll be going over there after I make a stop in town," he said.

The first stop Gonzalo made in town was the church. The evening service had already started, and there were a dozen or so congregants, so he entered as quietly as he could. He genuflected before the altar, catching Father Moreno's eye. Father Moreno used his chin to point toward the offices behind the altar.

The office Officer Vargas had chosen was windowless and small. It was fitted out with a desk, two chairs, and a filing cabinet, and there was barely room for the people who were supposed to make use of these pieces of furniture. When Gonzalo opened the door to the room, he hit Vargas, who was faithfully standing guard over his prisoner.

"Excuse me," the sheriff said as he squeezed his way past his deputy to a seat facing the prisoner. He could tell the prisoner was nervous and before speaking, Gonzalo decided to take advantage of that nervousness. He adopted a tone that seemed to reassure the prisoner that he was speaking with a friend while still reminding him that he had things to worry about.

"Now, I just have a few simple questions for you, but you have been read your rights, correct? Good. You know you don't have to say a word to me; we will get you a lawyer if you feel you need one. Do you understand all of this?"

The prisoner nodded yes.

"I need you to give your answer out loud. Do you understand your rights?"

"Yes."

"Good. Since you haven't asked for a lawyer, I'll start asking questions. First, very simple—what's your name?"

"Jose Salgado."

"Good. That matches the information on the papers you gave Officer Pareda, so we're off to a good start. Next, does the car you were stopped in belong to you?"

"Yes."

"Very good, that also matches the information in the papers you gave Officer Pareda. This next question is a little bit trickier; are you ready? Your driver's license says you live in Naranjito, yet you were found in one of the most remote parts of Angustias—what were you doing there? Do you have family in La Cola? Friends maybe?"

Jose didn't know how to answer this question. He, of course, knew no one who lived in La Cola.

"I got lost."

Gonzalo sat silently for a moment as though the information he had just heard needed some time to be fully absorbed and digested.

"That's it? You just got lost? You sure? Okay. I'll take your word for it, you were up in La Cola by accident. Another question, while you were up in La Cola, did you park your car, even for a few minutes?"

"No."

"Let me rephrase the question. While you were up in La Cola, did you park your car, blue Toyota Camry, 1986, in front of a little shack at the very top of the hill?"

"No."

"Let me rephrase the question again. Did you park in front of a little shack at the top of the hill where two of my officers were assaulted? Did you park at that crime scene?"

"No."

Gonzalo leaned back in his chair and crossed his arms. He pursed his lips and knit his brow as though he were deep in thought.

"Here's my problem, Jose. The car was parked in front of the shack where my officers were assaulted. It was parked in front of another house where another person was assaulted. It was parked in front of a house where a woman was killed. You say you were driving the car, getting lost in Angustias. I believe that part. You say you didn't do all this parking that I'm talking about. I don't think I should believe you about this. You look intelligent. What do you think? Should I?"

Jose licked his lips and knit his brow and sweat formed on his forehead though the room was cool. He fidgeted in his seat, and Gonzalo was on the verge of leaving his chair and letting Jose reconsider his options.

"I don't understand the question."

"This is not a game show, Jose. You can't get more time by having me repeat myself. The way you move, the way you sweat, this tells me you have something to say, but you don't want to say it. You would rather lie, but you can't think of anything. Am I right?"

Jose didn't answer. Instead he looked at the tops of his shoes.

"Let me make this easy, Jose. There was a murder. Elena Maldonado was stabbed seven times. Young woman, very pretty. She had a hard life and somebody ended it for her just one day after she became a mother. Can you imagine that? This animal was driving your car. Now I have two other guys in custody for this crime. We saw them with the same car you were in. Maybe you did it, maybe they did it. Who knows? Maybe you all did it. You don't want to talk to me? Fine. I'll ask them who they think did it."

Gonzalo got out of his chair, put it back where he had found it, told Vargas to watch the prisoner closely, adjusted his gun belt, and left the room. In all the time he gave Jose to stop him, the young man didn't even raise his head. The sheriff next headed for his station house.

CHAPTER FIFTEEN

Getting to Santurce was easier on the map than it was in life. The map shows a more or less straight line from Angustias to Santurce and the legend will say it is only a matter of something less than twenty miles. The first fifteen miles or so passed without incident for Deputy Estrada though the map lied. There was not a hundred yards of that road that did not have a turn in it. In fact, some twists were so pronounced that at times Estrada was actually headed back in the direction of Angustias. Still, the roads were clear, and he was able to drive comfortably above forty miles an hour. Had he traveled the road more often, he would have gone faster instead of being passed by several frustrated drivers.

The last five miles getting into Santurce were nightmarish. It was nearing six in the evening, but it was still rush hour. Natives to the area joked that the evening rush hour was only a continuation of the morning rush hour and the drivers lived in their cars. Estrada headed into what was called throughout the island *El tapon de Bayamon*, the Bayamon plug, named after the town where it all began each workday morning. Having spent most of his adult life on the southern side of the island, he had never encountered *El tapon* during its most ferocious though he had, of course, heard stories. He rounded a corner, merged into traffic and was horrified to find the stories were true.

There were drivers standing next to their cars having conversations with neighborhood residents sitting on their balconies. Street vendors were doing a brisk business having set up their carts with the knowledge that the drivers would get hungry and thirsty waiting to move forward a few yards. Having nothing better to do, Estrada counted the cars ahead of him in the lane. He could count off twenty, but he was sure the line was much longer, and when after five minutes of traffic he had moved something less than twenty feet, he began to think the line of cars was infinite.

In all this, there were few car horns heard. There was no place for cars to go. Even the sidewalks were narrow if one was inclined to drive along them. There was, however, the occasional, inevitable driver who switched lanes as often as possible in an effort to outwit all the other drivers. This caused most of the honking, as the rude stuck the nose of their cars into the tiniest of spaces between cars.

This also caused two slight accidents in the first

twenty minutes Estrada sat in his car. In one accident, one car sheared the passenger-side mirror off another car. Neither driver left his car, both apparently deciding the damage was the price of getting home. Instead, the driver at fault simply balled up a ten-dollar bill and tossed it through the other driver's open window, landing it in his lap. The driver stuffed it into his shirt pocket without bothering to straighten it out.

The other accident was more severe. The driver of a brand new, gray Porsche tried to nose his way in front of a twenty-five-year-old Chevrolet Impala. The Impala simply did not stop moving, and Estrada closed his eyes and scrunched down in his seat at the sound of impact.

"Five thousand in damage," he told himself.

That same thought apparently went through the Porsche owner's mind, and he jumped out of his car, fished a tire iron from the back and headed for the Impala. A police officer on a motor scooter flashed his lights and sounded his siren as he hurried to the accident weaving between the lanes. This froze the man in his tracks.

"Get back in your car," the officer commanded. When the man stayed where he was, the officer got off his scooter and moved toward him.

"He hit me," the man argued.

"You hit him. I saw the whole thing. Now unless this man wants you to fix his Impala, you need to get in your car and keeping moving along."

The man stood in the middle of the road a minute before deciding that he was not going to win the argument. He climbed back into his car muttering about the corruption of all police officers and of everyone else who worked for the government.

Nearly a half-hour later, Estrada walked into the precinct in Santurce.

"I need to speak with a Sergeant Romero," he said to the person manning the front desk. He was pointed toward double doors.

Sergeant Romero's desk was one of a row of four desks; it was the only one with anyone sitting at it, and it was the messiest desk. Sergeant Romero was in his fifties, with a large paunch that looked like it would be hard to the touch like a pregnant woman's can be. He had graying wavy hair that was slicked back violently, and he was halfway through a cigarette, a tall cup of coffee and a *cubano* sandwich of pork piled on pork with a hint of cheese.

"You're Estrada, right?"

"Yes."

Sergeant Romero took another bite of his sandwich, another gulp of his coffee, a last drag of his cigarette then sprang out of his chair, sucked in his gut to put on his gun belt, and motioned for Estrada to follow him. Though he walked quickly, he had a pronounced limp.

"It got shot off," he said as they left the building.

"Excuse me?"

"It got shot off. My leg. It got shot off. Line of duty."

"I'm sorry to hear that. . . ." Estrada had nothing else to say, but this didn't close the matter for Sergeant Romero.

"You were looking at my limp. I limp, you know. I was in a gun fight in '67. Three guys come out of a bank in Fajardo, I was off duty, I pulled out my weapon. I hit all three guys; they never hit me. Two of them fell right there, were taken to the hospital; they're still in jail. The third guy got away, got to the car, drove off, crashed, they took him to the morgue."

The two officers walked on in silence for a city block.

"In '87, I get called to a routine domestic violence run. I knew the woman. I knew the man. I had arrested him before. I had counseled the women ten times that she should leave the guy, run away. Anyway, I go into the house. She won't tell me where he is. She says she's scared. My partner and I start a search. I go into the bedroom. I don't see anything. He's under the bed with a shotgun. When I get close, he shoots me in the right shin."

Estrada began to wonder what he had done to have this nightmare inflicted on him, but then he checked himself. He had heard a dozen stories like this. They were all instructive. They were all for his own good.

"I hit the ground. I couldn't reach my gun even if I had thought about it, and I didn't think about it. That's the strangest thing. I grabbed my leg, but I didn't even think about grabbing my weapon. Anyway, the guy couldn't pump his shotgun—it was a pump action—because there wasn't enough room under the bed. My partner ran in and put six bullets into him through the mattress. He calls for an ambulance, for backup, for everything. Anyway, we're waiting. I think I'm dying. There's pain even when I breathe. The woman comes into the room, she's crying her eyes out. She sits on the ground, cradles her dead husband like a baby and says, 'I told you it wouldn't work.'"

Estrada knew he had just gotten his lesson.

"Can you believe that? It still gets me. It's been three years, and it still gets me. 'I told you it wouldn't work.' She's in jail now. Conspiracy. Anyway, the department wanted to get rid of me, but I get more if I can stick around for another thirteen months. They couldn't say no as long as I sit at the desk."

They rounded a corner. They were in what seemed to be the bad side of town. Here the houses were run-down. The porches were all fenced in and decorated with car furniture or sofas with torn cushions. Women and young girls stood on street corners and Estrada was sure some of them were prostitutes, unafraid of the approaching police.

They passed a car that had been stripped of all useful parts and burned. There was a red sticker affixed to what was its trunk indicating when the car was to be towed away.

"This is the house you want."

"Whose house is this?"

"Your sheriff said Elena Maldonado was killed, daughter of Perfecto Cruz. Her mother was from here, Santurce. Perfecto had friends here. . . ."

"You knew Perfecto?"

"Every police officer in Santurce knows Perfecto if he's on this job ten years. Perfecto loved Santurce. The bars, the prostitutes, the cock fights, the illegal gambling. I arrested him twice myself. Drunkenness. He was a wicked bastard. Drunk, he was worse. Anyway, if Perfecto was up to anything, his friends here know about it."

"No one said he was up to anything. He got religion before he died."

Sergeant Romero laughed a belly laugh that brought tears to his eyes as he pulled out a pair of black wires from his shirt pocket.

"Religion? You think God's gonna let something like that in heaven?"

Romero used the wires to pick the lock on the front gate of the house, then yelled out.

"Carlos! Come out here! We have to talk!"

A minute later a man in his twenties came out of the house and onto the porch. He was barefoot, wearing torn jeans and a sleeveless undershirt. His face needed a shave, his hair needed combing and Estrada was sure his whole body needed a wash.

"What do you want? I thought they kept you at a desk or something, Romero, you know, like a woman cop."

"Are you going to invite us in, or not?"

"I got nothing to say to you. I definitely don't have anything to say to a *gandule*. I didn't think *gandules* worked in the real cities."

Calling Estrada a green bean was a reference to his uniform color and to the fact that the officers in green usually only worked in small towns. Though they technically had the same rights and responsibilities as the officers in blue, *los metropolitanos*, the public often gave them less respect. *Los metropolitanos* also sometimes thought of the officers in green as country cousins.

"You should watch your tone, Carlos. Now come over here and let me in or I'll have to force my way in. You won't like it if I force my way in."

"You can't force your way in. That gate's too strong and you're too fat."

Carlos did a little dance on the other side of the gate.

"Come close, so I can catch you, and we'll see if you dance."

Carlos stupidly did as he was asked, doing a jig that brought him close but just out of reach. That's when Romero pushed open the gate, grabbed the young man and rammed him into the cement wall of the house. He gave Carlos a slap on the back with his forearm, bringing him down to the ceramic tiled floor. Estrada could see there was blood on the wall. He moved in close to offer his assistance, but Carlos was already as submissive as he was going to get.

"I told you, you wouldn't like it, Carlos. You should have opened the gate for me."

"I'm bleeding," Carlos said.

"Life is hard for a lot of people, Carlos. Come on, let's get inside."

Romero pulled Carlos to his feet, twisted his right arm behind his back and pushed Carlos into the house. Estrada followed.

Romero forced Carlos into a chair and stood over him.

"What did I do, Romero?"

"You? Probably nothing. I'm not here for you unless you give me trouble. I won't search this place for guns, for marijuana, for large, unexplainable sums of money . . . Unless I don't get cooperation."

"I don't have any of that here, man. I'm clean. . . ."

"Let me guess. You got religion. Look, I just need a little information. Give me what I want, and I get out of here. Lie to me, and it's going to be very painful for you. You understand?"

Carlos nodded yes.

"Good. Now. Perfecto Cruz was here in the last few months. Why?"

"How am I supposed to know?"

Romero took a step closer, and Carlos cringed.

"Let's try again. Perfecto was working on something, right?"

"Look man, the guy got religion. That's what he told me."

Romero smacked Carlos on the side of his head, toppling him and the chair he sat on. He stooped over Carlos and lifted him off the ground by his right upper arm. Estrada righted the chair.

"Let's get over this religion business. Is that okay with you, Carlos? I'm no priest. I don't talk about religion. I go to mass; the priest talks about religion. Now. One more time. What was Perfecto up to?"

"If you don't hit me again, I got something for you."

"Okay, if you got something good for me, I won't hit you again. If you lie to me, I'll hurt you. What have you got?"

"You're not going to believe me. . . ."

"I hope, for your sake, that I do."

"Perfecto was looking for a boyfriend for his daughter. This was a few months ago, maybe four or five months ago."

Romero looked to Estrada, wanting to find out if this was useful. Estrada nodded.

"Keep going. What do you mean, he was looking for her boyfriend?"

"Not for her boyfriend. He was looking for a boyfriend for her. He wanted to find someone who could be her boyfriend. He was trying to hook her up with someone decent."

"She's a married woman."

"He said he was going to take care of her husband. That her husband beat her."

"What do you mean, 'take care of'?"

"I don't know that. I think she was getting a divorce or something. Perfecto wanted someone she could marry after she got divorced."

"So who did he get?"

"Salgado. Jose Salgado. He's a young guy from around here. He hasn't been around for two or three years. He works as a ... something technical ... telephone company ... radio ... something like that. Perfecto said, he was going to contact Jaime Salgado, his father. That's the last I saw of Perfecto. I met Jaime a few weeks ago. He told me his son was getting together with Perfecto's daughter. That is all I know about Perfecto and his daughter."

After admonishing Carlos to be good and to take a bath, Romero led Estrada back onto the street.

"That's weird. I can't really imagine Perfecto as a matchmaker. Does any of this help you?"

"It confirms that she had a boyfriend. It gives us a name. It might be useful."

"Well, we have another stop to make. We'll see if we can get you a little to go back to Gonzalo with."

The two officers walked along in silence for a minute before Romero started another round of conversation.

"Did you think I was too rough with Carlos?"

"You know him better than I do. . . ."

"Carlos Feliciano is drug dealing scum. This is better than when he was pimping scum. But scum is scum. If you treat scum like something better, you will always regret it. . . . Here we are."

The two men walked into a bar. Like most bars, this place was dark, smelled of cigarettes more than alcohol, and had a handful of regulars getting down to the serious business of getting drunk. Romero walked up to one of the booths where there was a sole customer. The man looked up from his drink too late to get out of the booth before Romero got to him. The officer put a hand on his shoulder forcing him back into his seat as he tried to get up.

"I need to talk to you, Jaime. About your son."

"What son?" Jaime asked and regretted asking. Romero pushed his head down onto the table, squishing his face into the Formica, and pulled his right arm behind his back. The man looked up at Estrada.

"Are you going to let him abuse me like this?"

"I'm just here to support Officer Romero," Estrada explained. He crossed his arms.

"Now, Jaime. I know this position has to be uncomfortable for you. You see my belly? If you want me to let you go, tell me what I want to hear. If you don't tell me, I'm going to put this belly on your arm and I'm going to push with it. When you hear

something crack, that'll be your arm. You understand how this is going to go?"

"Got it."

"Good. Now tell me about Perfecto Cruz."

"What do you want to know?"

Romero pulled on the man's arm, which was now
in a position that Estrada felt sure could not be
within the normal range of motion.

"Try being a little more direct with your answers,
Jaime. It saves time."

"Perfecto came to me a few months ago. He was
looking for a boyfriend for his daughter. He said his
son-in-law was no good, she was looking for someone else. He said he was looking for a hardworking
man, clean-cut, wouldn't abuse her. I told him about
my son, Jose. He talked to Jose. Jose and the girl got
together. That's all I know."

"Where's your son now?"

"How'm I supposed to know?"

"Wrong answer."

Romero brought his belly close to Jaime's arm.
Estrada grimaced, awaiting the sound of breaking
bone, but Jaime cried out for mercy.

"Wait, wait, wait! Jaime works for a cable televi-
sion company in Naranjito. I think he's been rent-
ing a room there. I really don't know where. It's a
small town."

"What was Perfecto's scheme?"

"What scheme? He got religion," Jaime answered.

With that answer, Officer Romero pulled Jaime Salgado's head off the table and slammed it back down hard enough to make his bottle of beer bounce off the surface and onto the floor.

"This is my exercise for the day, Jaime. I could do this for hours. You want to tell me what kind of scheme he had running here, or do I have to get it from you the hard way?"

"No scheme. It's the truth, I swear. He told me he got religion. Anyway, we never worked together. We drank together. I'm the only one who gets schemes, not him. Perfecto just likes to get drunk and fight. . . ."

"Perfecto's dead, Jaime. They killed him with an ax in Angustias. Now I know he didn't just want a boyfriend for his girl just because he turned nice all of a sudden. What was the scheme."

"Look up my boy. He's never been in trouble. I sent him to college. He's not into schemes. Check him out. He's dating the girl. . . . They're going to get married when she divorces her husband. I swear, this is what he told me."

"She's dead, Jaime. Since it wasn't Perfecto, I guess it has to be your son. Thanks."

Romero shoved Jaime aside and walked away, Estrada following.

"My boy didn't do anything! Check him out. Jose keeps clean. He always has. Jose didn't do anything!" Jaime Salgado yelled after them, but the officers just kept walking.

Outside the two men started back toward the precinct.

"Can you really break an arm with your belly?" Estrada asked.

"I never tried. It just sounded scary. Jaime Salgado is pimping scum. He uses that bar like an office. Anyway, I don't know if any of this is going to help the investigation. I hope it does, but Gonzalo'll get his man no matter what. I've only heard of one case he couldn't crack. Little girl was murdered. She died in his arms. Terrible case."

Estrada had not yet heard the story of this crime and he imagined Romero had brought it up to teach him another lesson, but the sergeant said nothing more.

A few minutes later, Estrada was back in his car, on the road to Angustias, fighting traffic that was thinning but still strong.

CHAPTER SIXTEEN

Gonzalo parked in front of the station house. Before he could cross the town's plaza, Maria Garcia and Carmen Ortiz accosted him. Ortiz spoke first.

"I hear you had a talk with Marcos Maldonado."

"Where'd you hear that?"

"Never mind the source. Can I have a precis of what my client said, or will I have to wait for pretrial discovery?"

Gonzalo sighed. Maria Garcia was a real estate lawyer who filled in as a public defender when a suspect needed to be questioned quickly. Still, she provided her clients with a vigorous defense. Carmen Ortiz actually knew what she was doing and appeared to be no less tenacious.

"Let me see, if I can remember . . . After he waived his right to have counsel present, he told me he had nothing to do with the murder of his wife. He said I should look for her boyfriend, a person he

211

has been fully aware of for some time but about whom he has never bothered to do anything. That was the main body of his thoughts on this whole matter."

"Is my client free to return to his home?"

"In the first place, Counsel, your client isn't leaving his bed in the clinic anytime soon. Secondly, more importantly, though Angustias is a tiny town in the middle of nowhere, we are not so naive as to release prisoners because they say they're innocent. I have forty-eight hours to collect evidence to bring against him. Right now, I'm trying to conduct a series of interviews that might actually clear him."

"Can I see my client?"

"You can see him," Gonzalo said walking away. "I'll send a deputy to the clinic with you."

"That won't be necessary, Sheriff."

"Yes, it will."

Gonzalo retrieved the physical evidence he had collected from the trunk of his car before entering the precinct. Gomez and Estrada were waiting for him in the station house when he arrived. He spoke to Anibal Gomez first.

"Anything to report?"

"They yelled at me a lot. They want a lawyer. I didn't know what to say, so I said nothing."

"That's perfect. I've got a small job for you. The lawyer, Carmen Ortiz, is going over with Maria Garcia to speak with Marcos Maldonado at the clinic. I want you to go over and stand guard. Make sure only the lawyers and the medical staff gets to see him. You got that?"

"Sure thing, *jefe*."

"Don't call me *jefe*, Anibal."

"Yes, sir, *patron*," Anibal said, giving Gonzalo an exaggerated salute and a goofy grin before taking a spare car key from the lap drawer of Gonzalo's desk and leaving.

Gonzalo pinched the bridge of flesh between his eyes. He felt a strong headache was not too far, perhaps even a migraine. He looked to Estrada.

"Tell me you got something good from your trip to Santurce."

At the name of the town, both prisoners stood up in their cells.

"Yeah. I wrote it all out waiting for you." Officer Estrada pulled a sheet of folded, yellow, legal-pad paper from his shirt pocket and handed it to the sheriff. Gonzalo looked it over for a few minutes.

"And you believe what they told you?" he asked.

"Hard to say. I believe that's what he told them; I don't know whether he meant it."

"Religion, huh?"

"It's what they say."

Gonzalo folded the paper again and tapped it gently against his lips, losing himself in thought for a moment.

"How's your eye?" he asked, and the two prisoners sat down again, despairing of hearing more that concerned them.

"I think it's swelled completely shut. It doesn't hurt though."

"Do you want to go home?"

"I'll live. If you don't need me for a while, I'd love to get something to eat."

"Sure, sure. By all means. Take an hour."

Estrada left the station house, and Gonzalo placed a chair for himself directly in front of taller brother's cell.

"When do we get a lawyer?" Pedro started as Gonzalo opened his mouth to speak.

"Tomorrow."

"Tomorrow?"

"Well, this is a small town. We only have one good lawyer, and you killed her client, so she won't work with you."

"I didn't kill nobody. You got the wrong man. You watch. You won't have any case against me."

"What about the man you beat up in the Maldonado house? Don't you think that's going to keep you behind bars for a while?"

Here Pedro laughed.

"What's so funny?" Gonzalo asked.

"You think I beat up some old man? You going to take me to court about something like that?"

"It's a serious charge. Are you denying you had anything to do with beating up the man at the house of Marcos and Elena Maldonado?"

"Yeah, I deny it."

"Then what are you saying, you were born with those lumps on your head?"

"I fell. Look, if all you have is some charge about some old guy, I can tell you right now, no old man is going to testify against me. I guarantee it. . . . If that old guy you're talking about thinks he's going to testify, just let me talk a little sense into him. . . ."

Pedro laughed again. Gonzalo stood up slowly, walked behind the prisoner, pulled out his night-stick, brought it over his head and brought it down with all the force he had onto Pedro's fingers. Pedro jumped out of his seat, but Gonzalo sat him down again with a sharp rap on his shoulder.

"This is abuse!" Pedro yelled.

"This? This is nothing. You jump out of that chair again, and you'll see what I mean. That old man is my best friend in this world. You hurt him bad. I promise you two things. He will testify, and you will pay for what you did."

"I'm not talking anymore until I have a lawyer."

"Good. Then listen. When you talk to your lawyer tomorrow, try to come up for a reason for you being at the Maldonado house. We have evidence that you were there before the murder and after the murder. Explain that or I guarantee you will spend twenty-five years in jail."

"You got nothing. You got assault on the old man. I don't think you even have that. If I was there, then he hit me first. If I was there, he hit me with a frying pan. If I was there, I have a right to defend myself. . . ."

"You have no rights when you're a burglar. Get up. You're going back in."

Pedro tilted his head back and thought of his options. He could either stand and go back to his cell as he was told, or he could be defiant, stay seated and possibly get hit on the knuckles again. He got up calmly and walked to his cell.

Next, Gonzalo brought out Carlos Tejada. He also wore handcuffs behind his back.

"Sit."

Carlos nervously did as he was told.

"Good. Stand."

Carlos did that as well.

"Good. Who's in control?"

Carlos looked at the sheriff with wide eyes.

"I asked you who is in control—you or me?"

"You," Carlos hurried to say as though the thought of being in control was frightening to him.

"No digas na', imbecile," his brother warned from his cell.

"Do you drink beer?" Gonzalo asked.

Carlos hesitated in his reply.

"It's okay to tell me. Most young people drink even if they're not old enough to. Do you drink beer?"

"Yes . . . sometimes . . ." Carlos seemed to ask Gonzalo what the right answer might be.

"Do you drink this brand?"

Gonzalo brought the crime-scene beer bottle out of the shopping bag and put it on his desk.

Carlos looked to his brother who shrugged back at him. Carlos said "no," and Gonzalo could see he was telling the truth.

"I drink Corona," the young man said simply.

"So I won't find your fingerprints anywhere on this bottle?"

"I don't think so. . . ."

"But you're not sure?"

"I never touched that bottle."

Gonzalo sat silently for a moment. Neither brother seemed to have any reaction to the sight of the bottle. Earlier they had as much as admitted that they had left some evidence at the scene. Apparently, this bottle wasn't it. Gonzalo reached into his shopping bag again, this time pulling out the murder weapon in its plastic evidence bag. The blood from the knife had smeared somewhat on the inside of the bag, and its brown wooden handle had stained where the blood had soaked through.

"How about this? Will I find your prints on this?"

Carlos Tejada's eyes had widened on seeing this, so Gonzalo knew he had seen it before.

"You're not answering me. Maybe the question is too hard. Have you ever seen this knife before?"

Carlos still had nothing to say.

"Still nothing? Let me give you a little history about this knife. We found it at the crime scene. It was put into the chest and belly of Elena Maldonado seven times. It caused her death. The person who left fingerprints on it will be charged with murder. If two people left fingerprints on it, two people will be charged with murder. You understand how this works?"

"I didn't do it. . . ." was all Carlos Tejada could say.

"*No digas na'*," his brother ordered from his cell.

"I'm not going to tell you anything . . ." Carlos told Gonzalo in a tone that sounded something like a question.

"That's fine with me. It will look better when I get a conviction for two brothers. This will put me in the newspapers. I know that sounds a little vain, but it really does help the city. If we get more publicity, we can ask for an increase in funding from the state. . . . You know how it goes." Gonzalo shrugged, and Carlos nodded as though he really did know how the Angustias police force fell in the state budget plans.

"Look. Let me inform you of what's going to happen next. I've got someone at the Maldonado home looking for more evidence. I'm going to get an officer here with a kit for lifting fingerprints. We'll look at the knife. We'll look at the bottle. We'll look at everything that was left behind at the Maldonado home. Then we're going to start matching your prints to the prints we find. That takes some time; we might have to go to Ponce—

they have a computer that does a better job than I can with a magnifying glass—anyway. Once I go to Ponce—listen to me, this is the important part—once I go to Ponce, I won't want to hear anything you have to say. You understand? Until I go to Ponce, you can confess, tell me what you know, et cetera. After that, your lawyer will tell you what to do. No deals then, okay?"

"What kinds of deals?" Carlos asked.

"*No digas na'*," his brother demanded again.

"Your brother is right. With all the evidence I have to collect, I don't have time to talk with you."

Gonzalo grabbed Carlos by his right upper arm, yanked him out of his chair and pushed him back into his cell. He went to a small table near his desk and turned on a radio and the station house CB. He kept the volume low and spoke into it at a whisper to avoid being heard by his prisoner though, in fact, they showed no interest in his conversation.

"Hector, are you out there?"

"Right here, boss."

"Where are you?"

"At the Maldonado house."

"Is Calderon still there?"

"Yeah."

"Have you guys found anything yet?"

"We've turned the bedroom inside out and upside down, but no luck yet."

Gonzalo had thought for months that Hector and Iris Calderon might be in the beginning stages of a romance, and the thought of the two young deputies in a house alone together passed through his mind and sent a chill down his spine. He had heard of office romances turning precincts into purgatories, and he wanted nothing to do with anything like that.

"Well, bring the fingerprint kit over here and anything you've found."

"Got it. Oh, Officer Calderon wants to know if she's going to be relieved anytime soon. She's been here for a long time and is getting—"

"She'll be relieved within an hour, Hector. I'll send Officer Estrada when he comes in."

Gonzalo put the CB aside for a moment and tried to think of all the areas in the investigation where he still needed more information. It turned out it was nearly every. He still had no idea where, exactly, the boyfriend fit in. He was pretty sure the two guys locked up in his precinct had something to do with Elena's murder, but he wasn't positive yet that they had actually killed her. Even if fingerprints proved that one of them had killed her, he still had no idea why. Was Marcos mixed up in this? Did he hire them to kill her out of jealousy? Perfecto found a boyfriend for Elena, but was he involved in all this in any other way? So far, the investigation had only gone from clear and simple when Marcos was found with the knife in hand, to a mess.

He picked up the CB again.

"Estrada, where are you?"

"Cafetin Lolita. Do you need me?"

"Have you eaten yet?"

"I'm in the middle."

"When you're done can you go over to the Maldonado house? I need you to watch the house while Calderon gets a break."

"Sure thing. I'll be over there in . . . fifteen minutes."

"That's great. Thanks."

The sheriff's next call was to Anibal Gomez at the clinic.

"How are things going over there, Anibal?"

"They're fine. The two woman lawyers left about five minutes ago. Marcos said he didn't need a lawyer. He threw them out. Do you still want me to make sure he doesn't talk to anyone else?"

"Has anyone else tried to talk to him?"

"He's asleep. Sedated, I think. Doctor said he could talk again in the morning."

"Good. Get back here and watch these prisoners."

"Will do, *jefe*."

Waiting for his deputies to arrive, Gonzalo began looking through his file cabinet. There was nothing specific that he wanted, but he felt he had to give his prisoners not only a show of diligence but a show that he knew exactly what his next steps were going to be and that he wasn't afraid to take them. The rifling through the files also gave him something to do while he waited.

Hector brought with him a series of white cards

with lifted fingerprints taped to them. Each card was carefully marked with when and where it had been taken.

"Here's the bottle. Here's the weapon." Gonzalo said, handing Hector each item in its clear plastic bag. "We'll talk about the results later."

Hector cleared off a space at his desk, slipped on latex gloves, and started to examine the items Gonzalo had given him using a magnifying glass. Both brothers sat up in their cells, watching Hector work on the material evidence.

"What's he doing?" Carlos asked.

Gonzalo stared at him a moment, then turned away, making a point of ignoring the prisoner. If either brother was going to break, it was bound to be Carlos, so the more nervous he was, the better.

When he was done getting what prints he could from the two objects, Hector took out a small camera from his desk drawer and photographed both sides of the knife several times.

"Why's he doing that?" Carlos asked. No one even looked his way this time.

Hector rebagged both items carefully, then went to the bottom drawer of the file cabinet nearest him. He took out a large black binder and began to leaf through it. After a few minutes he stopped and compared a note card fingerprint with one in the book. He pointed out his finding to Gonzalo.

"Wow. No kidding. I'm going to have to head out there. Stay with these guys a couple of minutes.

When Calderon or Gomez comes in, I need you to go over to the church and take prints from the prisoner we have there."

Gonzalo went out into the sunlight, which, at almost eight in the evening was finally dying away. He checked his flashlight, then got into his car and drove away.

As soon as Gonzalo pulled away, Hector picked up the ringing phone in the precinct.

"Is anyone going to take this prisoner out of here, or do I have to stay with him all night?" Jorge Nuñez was on the other end of the line, and he sounded irate.

"I don't know what to say. . . . Sheriff Gonzalo just left. The case is beginning to come together, but we have to keep everybody separate. . . ."

"Can someone else come to watch this guy? I'm tired of baby-sitting him."

"What's he doing now? I mean is he acting violently?"

"He's drooling!"

"I'll try to get someone over there in ten to fifteen minutes, okay?"

"Well, make it quick. I want to go home."

The deputy mayor hung up the phone on his end, and at that moment Anibal Gomez came in through the door.

"Anibal, I need you to go to the *alcaldia*."

"What for?"

"Somebody has to watch Marrero." Hector saw

through the corner of his eye that both brothers sat up with wide eyes at the mention of the name.

"Marrero? Can't we just let him go home for the night and rearrest him first thing in the morning?"

"Nope. Nuñez says he's been talking up a storm. Says its pretty interesting stuff and he wants a deputy there to record it, so here. Take the tape recorder. Make sure the batteries work. Good."

Hector handed Anibal a micro tape recorder and watched as the brothers knit their brows and worried.

CHAPTER SEVENTEEN

The day had been uncomfortable. Being a tropical island, one expected heat and humidity in Puerto Rico, so there was no reason to complain there, but the activity of the day—though none of it was particularly strenuous—wore heavily on Gonzalo, and he felt wasted.

He drove slowly toward the Maldonado home, catching the twilight breeze on the arm he dangled out his car window. The air was beginning to cool and, though it had not been oppressive, he was grateful for the drop of a few degrees. As he pulled onto the patch of lawn in front of the home that had been receiving police vehicles for the last several hours, he paid attention to the chorus of grasshoppers and *coquis* that welcomed the coming of night. He knew that soon bats would swoop across the sky, abandoning their daytime shelter, and owls would start asserting their presence. In another hour, Mari's favorite *telenovela* would come on. He wondered if she would set the baby aside long enough to watch it.

Officer Estrada came out onto the porch as Gonzalo was parking. He waited for the sheriff to step onto the porch before speaking.

"Why are we looking for something here?" he asked.

Gonzalo paused a moment before answering. He had been hoping to uncover something either missing or recently placed in the house since the attack on Collazo, and the question seemed almost like a trick.

"Well, the guy came here. He beat up Collazo. I don't think he came here for sightseeing. He was in the bedroom; he was ignoring the body. He wanted something—either to take something or to leave something behind, something that would implicate someone else in the murder, I think—"

"Exactly, that's what he came here for, but if he found what he was looking for, then he took it with him. If he wanted to plant evidence, maybe Collazo kept him from doing that. . . ."

"Then he still has it."

"I wouldn't say that. I imagine he could have gotten rid of it in the time it took us to find him."

"But it might still be in the Toyota or in the shack he was using. . . ."

"Or anywhere he drove to after getting out of

here. Or it might have been thrown into a fire or a garbage can or sold. For all we know whatever it was was fed to a dog."

"Still, we have to treat this object like it's something we can find. Stay here. Keep looking around. For all we know it's still here."

Gonzalo started to walk back to his car.

"Sheriff . . . Did you come here for something specific?"

"Oh, yeah . . . Calderon thinks I treat you like a second-class citizen. . . . Maybe I do. Have you felt that?"

Estrada searched his memory for a moment, then shrugged and shook his head.

"I get treated like a deputy. That's my job."

"Well, that's what I thought, but she thought I had something against you. . . ."

"Well, you don't like the fact that I pay so much attention to my looks. . . ."

"I never said that."

"You don't have to. I can see it every time I comb my hair or put on my sunglasses. But I have to do that. I'm past forty and divorced. I want to get married someday, and I won't get a woman to look at me if I don't take care of myself. Maybe you took better care of your looks before you got married."

The vision of himself putting pomade in his hair, slicking it back and ironing his shirts in the days

227

when he was wooing Mari ran through Gonzalo's mind. He nodded.

"Look. I know I make a fool out of myself sometimes. That's the game I have to play. Who knows when I'll run into the next Mrs. Estrada?" Estrada smiled.

"Okay. Just thought I'd clear that up. I don't mean to leave you out of anything in this department. For the record, you've been doing a great job today, and everything's been fine so far."

When Gonzalo had climbed back into his car and driven away, Estrada shook his head, took off his sunglasses and laughed out loud.

"At least, I attracted someone's attention," he said to himself, then he went back into the house and continued a slow, methodical search for he knew not what.

Gonzalo's next stop was El Colmado Ruiz. Ruiz was sitting behind the counter as usual. He had a small, black-and-white TV on, and he was laughing at a comedy. He was alone and he turned off the TV as Gonzalo approached the counter and the comedy cut to a commercial.

"Do you have Budweiser here?"

"Sure." He got up and headed for a double-door refrigerator he kept behind the counter with him out of the reach of the public.

"No, no. I don't want one. I'm on duty. I just wanted to know if you sold them. Did you sell any today?"

"What's this about, Gonzalo? I don't sell to minors, you know that. If they're not sixteen they don't get a bottle or even a cup of beer from me."

"The drinking age is eighteen."

"That's what I meant. If they're not eighteen, they get nothing."

"It's not about minors. Did you sell a beer recently to Perfecto Cruz?"

The store owner reacted to the question as though it had been a slap in his face. He stepped back, his eyes wide, and tensed up. Even with so obvious an overreaction, Gonzalo could tell Ruiz was going to deny selling the beer as soon as he got over the shock and was able to put words together again.

"Perfecto's got religion. I mean he had it. . . . He doesn't drink anymore. . . ."

"What I asked you was whether you sold him a beer recently. I don't care if Perfecto's got the Holy Ghost. I didn't even say he drank the beer. Did you sell him one?"

"I'm not mixed up in any of this. . . ."

"I didn't say you were mixed up in anything. You're not going to go to jail for selling a beer. Did you sell—"

"Yes! Stop it! I sold him the beer! I didn't do anything else. I didn't even know about the girl."

Detective work was often like putting together a thousand-piece jigsaw puzzle. Usually a few pieces fell into place fairly easily; recovery of the victim's body, often the recovery of the weapon. Other pieces were harder to match. This one small bit of information—that Perfecto had bought a beer that wound up in the Maldonado home—had been easy enough to pry out of the storekeeper. Placing this one piece, however, showed that there might be many others he was unaware of. Certainly Ruiz knew more than he would say.

"Tell me about the sale of the beer, Ruiz."

"I know nothing . . ."

"Don't get me angry. What do you mean, 'I know nothing'? Of course you know something. How much did the beer cost?"

"One dollar. That's what all the beers cost. That I know."

"When did Perfecto buy it?"

"This morning. That I know."

"Who was he with when he bought it?"

"I don't know . . ."

Gonzalo reached for his nightstick. He would not have used it on the storeowner in a million years—he liked Ruiz—but he figured the threat would be enough to get more information.

"He was with a young guy. With the guy Marrero was fighting with. A *morenito*. Your deputies saw him . . ."

"Did you ever see that guy here before?"

"A couple of times. No more than that, I swear. I sold him some Budweisers. That's all he takes. Always just one, never a six-pack. Always a bottle, never a can. He always takes it, he never drinks it here."

"Did Perfecto always come with him?"

"Nope. Never. Just today."

"Did Perfecto start drinking here again a few months ago?"

"He came in once in a while. He told me to open a tab, so I did. He had a couple beers a week on his tab. No hard drinks. The beer today was on his tab. He's dead, right?"

"Very dead."

"He didn't leave twenty-six dollars behind, did he?"

"Maybe. I'll check for you in a couple of days." Gonzalo pulled away from the counter.

"One more thing."

"What? I always cooperate with the police, you know that."

"Yes, I know. But the sign on the register says you don't let people run up tabs. Is it true or not?"

"It's true, but Perfecto is . . . was a special case."

"Why?"

"Well, Sheriff. People say he got religion. He said he had religion, he drank beer and told me about Hell. . . . But I don't care if he got religion or not. I remember when he had no religion. He would put a knife in someone like I put a knife in a *pernil*. Perfecto Cruz wants a tab, I give him a tab. You understand? For safety."

"You could just call me—"

"Not if he stabs me."

Gonzalo nodded and left the store.

Outside the air was turning cool and the sky was darkening. Stars were making their appearance in great numbers. Gonzalo took a look at them before getting into his car. The thought crossed his mind that on some distant planet there could be a sheriff trying to work out a murder case just like the one he was working on. Then he reminded himself that the stars he was looking at were many light-years away so that the case the alien sheriff was working on was either solved already or completely cold. He shook his head to clear these foolish thoughts and got into his car.

Gonzalo's next trip was to the home of Perfecto Cruz. He tried to think of good legal reason to enter the home without the owner's consent, without even having tried to contact any relatives. Then he reminded himself that this was the Cruz family and that not one of them would care about Perfecto's death or his house unless money was left to them.

The door to the shack that Perfecto had called home was padlocked. Gonzalo used his nightstick to pry the lock off the door. The house had only two distinct sections to it—the front room and a kitchen area separated from the front by a plywood wall that ran most of the way from one side of the structure to the other. The gap where the plywood didn't touch the wall was the threshold.

To say the decor of the house was spartan would

have been to mock. Clothes hung from several nails in the wall. The front room had a wooden chair, a night table with two drawers and a hammock. Both ends of the hammock were hanging from the same hook—this constituted making the bed. There were no pictures, no radio, no newspaper lying about, nothing.

The kitchen had a sink, a dish, a spoon, a cup. Gonzalo figured that any cooking had to go on outside over an open flame, and he guessed that any pots or pans would be outside as well.

"I would have killed myself too," Gonzalo said, then he slapped his own lips harshly to remind himself he was speaking of a fellow human being.

He pulled latex surgical gloves from his back pocket and put them on to search the home. He went to the night table and searched the drawers finding nothing but underclothes and a small plastic tray with a bar of soap and a half-used Right Guard. He pulled the drawers all the way off their tracks to make sure nothing was taped underneath or shoved in behind them. Nothing was.

Next he checked the clothes hanging on the nails. In all the pockets combined there were nine dollar bills, a black plastic comb, a Bic pen, and three or four scraps of paper with phone numbers and names scribbled onto them. None of the names and numbers rang any bells with Gonzalo. He folded the papers and put them in his shirt pocket.

Behind the house, the dense covering of tree

branches and leaves kept out the waning sunlight and Gonzalo had to turn on his flashlight. In a space between three trees, he found the cooking area he had suspected. There was a small pile of kindling, and two cinder blocks with a piece of metal grating laid across formed the stove. There was a skillet on the grate, and a pot was hung by its handle from a nail stuck into one of the trees.

Gonzalo made his way to the shed behind the house where he had spoken to Perfecto earlier in the day. This shack was almost as large and as old as the house itself, but it had no windows. The door here was also padlocked, and Gonzalo pried this lock off as well. What was inside the shack stunned the sheriff.

Though Perfecto's property had not had working electricity since he stopped paying the electric bill some years earlier, in the shack was a treasure trove of all sorts of electrical appliances—TVs and VCRs, toasters and toaster ovens, four air conditioners stacked one on top of the other, radios and CD players both portable and stationary. There was a shelf of twenty or so car radios. Most items were still in their packaging; some other things were slightly used. The thought passed through Gonzalo's mind that the items in the room would probably clear up a couple dozen police investigations.

A shoe box on one of the shelves contained a pound or two of jewelry—torn necklaces, inscribed watches, wedding and engagement rings.

"Religion," Gonzalo muttered.

He closed the shed and made his way back to his car. He sat behind the wheel for a few minutes trying to think of what to do next. It seemed to him that Perfecto had played a larger than expected role in the murder of his own daughter. Perfecto may have been at the scene of the murder. He might have hired someone to kill her; he might have done it himself. He was certainly back in the business of crime. . . . Hector's voice on the CB interrupted his train of thoughts.

"I've got more fingerprint results for you."

"Can you talk to me about it where you are?"

"Sure. I'm outside the station house. . . . Officer Calderon is with the prisoners; Vargas is in the *alcaldia*; he said he was getting claustrophobic in the church office. . . ."

"Okay, look. Bring me the fingerprint information at the house in La Cola. Bring a strong flashlight or two and the evidence kit."

"Okay, I'll be there in seven minutes."

"No racing. It's getting dark out."

"Okay, then I'll see you in nine minutes."

Gonzalo got to the house in La Cola a minute before his deputy. He was able to watch a part of Hector's ascent along the winding roads and though he would have been afraid for any other driver, he knew Hector was about as good a driver as there was in Angustias, probably in all of Puerto Rico. He had been in a dozen car chases in his time as an officer—mostly drag racers who liked the challenge of the unbusy, winding roads in Angustias. He had caught everyone he had gone after so far except for one who had shot out the front tire of the motorcycle Hector had commandeered. That was the only occasion when Hector had hurt himself driving. Otherwise, he was the safest driver even at speeds exceeding a hundred miles an hour.

"What have you got for me?" Gonzalo asked his deputy even before he had turned off the car engine.

"Just where I think the knife came from. We have two prints from Maldonado in the blood on the handle. Of course, we expected that, but we also have two partials from Perfecto Cruz on the blade; they're in a position that makes it look like he was giving the knife or receiving it by the blade. Some of it was smudged by the stabbing, but we have enough to identify."

"Great. The father kills his own daughter."

"Well, to be sure we just have to match the knife to others in his kitchen, right?"

"That's not going to happen." Gonzalo explained all he had found at the home of Perfecto Cruz.

"He was warehousing stolen goods? Does that sound like him? I never knew him, but I thought he was more of an opportunist than a planner like that."

"Oh, yeah. This wasn't his idea. In fact, if we find

236

whose idea it was, I think we find the person who wanted Elena Maldonado dead."

"Then what are we doing looking here?" Hector asked.

"We're leaving no stone unturned. That's our job."

CHAPTER EIGHTEEN

Father Moreno was sitting on one of the rear pews when Anibal Gomez walked into the church, tape recorder in hand.

"You're here to relieve the other officer?"

"They told me the prisoner wants to talk. I'm here to get what he has to say."

"Who told you the prisoner wants to talk?"

"God," Anibal said with a pronounced wink that Father Moreno did not know how to interpret.

"Oh . . . well, let me show you to him."

Father Moreno walked to the offices at the back of the church with Anibal following close behind. He opened the door on Officer Vargas and Jose Salgado, who were sitting only three or four feet apart in the tiny office, staring at each other.

"Jose, you wanted to tell the officer something?" Father Moreno started.

"I did?" Jose replied. He of course knew nothing of what Hector had told Anibal.

"That's what I understand."

At these words, Jose Salgado had something of an attack of conscience. He knew himself to be a sinful man and wanted to erase his faults.

"Can I confess something to you?"

"Of course, my child. What is it?" It took Father Moreno a moment to realize that the prisoner was serious in his request. He asked the officers to leave the room.

"We can't leave you alone with a prisoner," Anibal started, but Father Moreno raised an eyebrow.

"We are in a church and I am a priest. A man has asked me to hear his confession and there is no power on Earth to stop me."

Father Moreno put his hand on the top of the backrest of the chair Officer Vargas was sitting on, and Vargas took this motion as a sign that he should leave the room. Anibal, seeing no way to support his position, followed within seconds.

Father Moreno took the seat Officer Vargas had been sitting in and faced the prisoner.

"I am ready to hear your confession, my son. God is ready to forgive you."

Now that the priest sat across from him, Jose Salgado had trouble saying anything. He looked down to his shoes, and Father Moreno could tell the was a struggle of conscience going on in Jose's soul; he had seen this same struggle many times before played out on the faces of the *Angustiados* who were his parishioners.

"It might help to start from the beginning," Father Moreno offered.

"That won't help, Father. It all looks bad to me."

"Then skip most of it and tell me what is the end of it all. Sometimes it works to go backwards. . . . You see how it could work?"

Jose nodded. It was clear that all parts of the story he had to tell were painful to him.

"My father is not a good Catholic. . . . He didn't raise me. . . . My mother raised me a good Catholic . . ."

Jose paused here, and Father Moreno felt he had to prompt him or risk having him stop here altogether.

"When was your last confession, my son?"

"It has been months since I confessed. I don't know when. Too long." Jose started to cry, and Father Moreno prompted him again.

"Speak. God is ready to forgive you."

"I fell in love, Father . . . With a married woman . . ."

"Did you consummate this . . . relationship?"

Jose looked up at Father Moreno and appeared confused.

"Consummate? No. She was a married woman. I wanted to, but she was pregnant . . . No. I did worse than that . . . I did worse . . ."

"What did you do, my son?"

"I don't know, Father . . . I don't know. I learned

of things . . . evil things . . . I learned of plots against this woman . . . evil things . . ."

"And what did you do, my son? What did you do when you learned of these plots?"

"I did nothing . . . That is my sin, Father . . . I did nothing . . . I was afraid, Father . . . I was afraid for myself, Father . . . I was afraid for myself . . . I let these plans be carried out, and I was afraid, Father . . . And I am still afraid . . ."

Here Jose Salgado lowered his head and broke down into tears, and Father Moreno reached across and put his arm on the younger man's back willing him to cry out his tears until he was no longer drowning inside.

Outside the office, Anibal debated with Vargas about how long the priest had been with the sinner.

"Moreno could be dead already. . . . I'm going in there."

He headed for the door, but Vargas put his hand on his chest and stopped his motion.

"That's a confession, Gomez. You can't go in."

"It's police business . . ."

"Not during a confession. You wait until Father Moreno comes out. The prisoner is secure."

Vargas said all this with such force that Anibal sat down on one of the pews, shaking his legs rhythmically to release his nervous energy.

"I'm going to the station house. When Father Moreno is finished, go in there and record anything

Salgado wants to say. If he doesn't want to say anything, just watch him. You understand me?"

"You don't outrank me."

"That's not what I asked you."

"I understand."

Vargas left the church and went to the station house where, after a drink of water and a trip to the bathroom, Hector gave him orders to relieve Jorge Nuñez in the *alcaldia*.

"Thank God," the deputy mayor said when Vargas walked in. "I thought I was going to have to listen to this guy all night. Here are the keys; give them to Gonzalo whenever you're done with this place." He put on a straw hat and shook the deputy's hand vigorously.

"I trust the investigation is coming along?"

"I think so," Vargas answered.

"Good. I'll talk to Gonzalo later. My wife cooked pork chops," Nuñez said in explanation, and he rushed out.

Vargas took a turn around the room. He had been inside the deputy mayor's office once before to report on a crime, but he was curious about the pictures on the wall behind the desk, and he did not want to sit with Marrero. Marrero, however, was feeling talkative.

"Is the investigation over? Is everyone in jail?"

"Who should be in jail, Marrero?"

"I don't know . . . I shouldn't be in jail . . ."

"You're not in jail."

"Good. Can you take these off?"

Each of Marrero's wrists was adorned with a set of handcuffs, which were attached to the armrests of the chair he sat in.

"Sorry. Those stay on until we have space in the prison to take you back."

"I want to go home."

"You attacked a little girl and a police officer. I think your chances of getting home this year are pretty low."

"I left something on the stove; my house can burn down."

"You live in a shack."

"It has sentimental value . . . Look, I have information. If you let me go, I'll tell you what I know."

"You have information that could help the investigation of the murder of Elena Maldonado?"

"Yeah, man. I know everything . . ."

"You're not just drunk, are you?"

"Drunk? I haven't had a drink in . . . oh my God . . . How many hours has it been?"

"Six or seven."

"Oh my God . . . I think I'm suffering from . . . from . . . what's that thing when you stop drinking?"

"Withdrawal?"

"That's it. Look, I have information. . . ."

"Tell me."

"What do I get?"

"I can guarantee you that if Gonzalo solves this

on his own, you're not going to get anything. If you have something to say, you might as well say it and maybe Gonzalo will charge you with something less."

Marrero smiled to himself and shook his head.

"No deal. Not even Gonzalo can figure this one out. This one's a knot. This one's a mess. I bet you a hundred dollars he doesn't figure this one out . . ."

Vargas walked back to the pictures on the wall. They were family pictures.

For his part, Gonzalo was trying to work out the mystery of Elena's death without help. If there was one failing above all others that Gonzalo himself would point out about his police work, it was the fear of not being able to figure out a mystery on his own. Part of this fear stemmed from the fact that he had been the first police officer Angustias had ever hired, and he spent the first ten years of his career working alone.

But there was also the fear that the *Metropolitanos* would swoop down from the San Juan or Ponce areas in their blue uniforms and take over an investigation he had started. They were entitled to do so according to the guidelines the police in Puerto Rico worked by. This would only add to the cachet of the *Metropolitanos* and the denigration of the officers who wore green, *Los Locales*.

This investigation, however, was more personal than that. He had driven Elena home, hadn't he? He had driven her to her death. Had he only listened to his wife and taken Elena to his house, she would be alive, she would have dodged the fatal knife. These thoughts stayed in the back of his mind throughout the long hours of the investigation—he wanted to solve the problem because he felt he had done something to cause the problem. These thoughts stayed in his mind though no one else thought anything like this, and everyone else would have been shocked to know he felt this way.

With Hector right behind him, Gonzalo entered the house in La Cola. Like Perfecto's house, there wasn't much to the structure and there was less to the furnishing. There was a front room with a table and two chairs. On the table there was a large Sultana cracker can. It was the type of can that often got opened up and flattened out in order to patch rusted-through areas of zinc roofs. Both officers, in fact, had seen entire houses sheeted in these cans.

Inside the can there was a light blue T-shirt. Gonzalo pulled it out and put it on the table. A small part of it was charred; the rest was covered with blood. Further down in the can, there was a small bundle of papers and envelopes held together with a rubber band. These also were partially burned, but the bulk of them appeared unharmed. Beneath them there were the ashes of other papers that had burned completely and a matchbook that had apparently been used to set the fire.

"This is probably what they were arguing about when we got here."

"What? The papers?"

"No. The fire. The can doesn't have any air holes in it. When they put the shirt in, they put out the fire. Maybe they were arguing about how to run this fire."

"That's a stretch."

"I like to call it a theory."

"Well, whatever it is, let's get this in bags."

"Where do you want to examine this stuff?"

"In the station house."

"In front of the brothers?"

"Hey, maybe they know something about these things that they'd like to share. . . ."

"Isn't it a risk to show them what we have right away? Shouldn't we—"

"I'm tired of these guys. They're going to see this stuff sooner or later. I've got to take them to San Juan tomorrow—they want lawyers—before they go, I'm going to know why Elena Maldonado died."

The two men bagged the evidence and took it out to the trunk of Gonzalo's car.

"You could just take them to Comerio," Hector said, and he smiled. The sheriff of Comerio was nearly sixty, but he was built along the lines of a baby bull and he was never more in his element than when he was beating a suspect to the edge of unconsciousness and then over the edge.

"Don't tempt me."

On the way back to the precinct, Gonzalo tried to think of how he should approach the brothers—should he play one off against the other? Should he offer one leniency for speaking against the other? Should he show them the evidence separately? Perhaps he should follow Hector's advice and hide the evidence from them, get them talking about evidence they thought they had destroyed. But he could not get out of his mind that the brothers should be confronted as directly as possible. That is what he did.

"Calderon, pick up," he called into his CB.

"Calderon's here."

"I'm coming in with some more evidence. Clear off my desk and put on some latex gloves."

CHAPTER NINETEEN

Gonzalo strode into the station house with two clear plastic bags of evidence. One contained the bloody T-shirt; the other had the half-burned papers. Calderon was waiting for him with a cleaned-off desk and latex gloves on. The brothers sat up in their cells.

"*Idiota*," Pedro muttered to his brother.

Gonzalo looked up at the prisoners as he was about to set the bags on his desk.

"Good," he said. "Start fighting each other. That's exactly what I want to see."

He placed the bag containing the shirt on the part of the desk that was closest to the cells and spilled the contents of the other bag on the desk.

"Here. Go through these. Look for phone numbers, names, etc. Show me anything you think is interesting. This is what they were going to plant in the Maldonado house. Next . . ." He pulled Perfecto's papers from his shirt pocket and handed them to Calderon. "See what matches in these papers, if anything."

"I want a lawyer now," Pedro spoke out, but Gonzalo ignored him.

"Hector, I'm getting an idea . . . Call Estrada. He's at the Maldonado house. Tell him to come over here and help Calderon."

"What do you want me to do?"

"When they're done, get some prints off the papers. Until then, get yourself something to eat."

With these instructions, Gonzalo left, crossing the plaza to the church. In the church, he found Anibal pacing up and down the center aisle.

"Where's your prisoner?"

"He's in one of the offices, chief . . ."

"Didn't I tell you not to leave a prisoner alone unless—"

"He's confessing to Father Moreno. Vargas told me not to interrupt."

"Well, okay. I guess a confession is an emergency. . . . How long has he been confessing?"

"Forever."

"You couldn't give me a more useful answer, could you?"

"Twenty minutes. Thirty maybe."

"That's better."

Gonzalo walked to the office door and, hearing nothing from within, he knocked.

Father Moreno answered the door and stepped out.

"I heard the prisoner's been in a confessing mood. Anything you'd like to share, Father?"

Father Moreno ignored Gonzalo's request.

"How can I help you, Sheriff?"

"Can I speak with the prisoner?"

"He has confessed to me, and I have warned him against speaking to you or any other law enforcement officer without an attorney. . . ."

"Did he kill Elena Maldonado?"

"Sheriff, I'm not going to discuss what he confessed. . . ."

"Father, by saying that, you are admitting that he confessed that he killed her. . . . Is that what you mean? Did he confess the murder?"

Father Moreno was perplexed about how to answer the question without revealing what had gone on during confession. Gonzalo came to his rescue.

"Look, Father. I'm sorry to put you in this kind of spot, but I came to the church thinking that Jose Salgado did not commit the murder. I came here thinking that the murderer is in a cell in the precinct. Now it sounds like he's in your office. My question is simp—"

"He needs a lawyer. Trust me, Sheriff, it is not as simple as you think."

Gonzalo stood, thinking whether he should pursue the issue any further, then he turned and left.

His next stop was the house of Maria Garcia.

He knocked and Maria answered in a bathrobe and slippers; she was clearly not happy to be disturbed.

"I'm sorry to bother you, but I need your assistance. Or Carmen Ortiz, if she is still around."

"Carmen left an hour ago. I think she felt pretty bad that she came all the way out here and—"

"Tell Ms. Ortiz I'm very sorry we could not put her to better use, but I've got work for you right now. . . ."

"Sheriff, I can't work this case; you know my reasons."

"I don't want you to actually work the case. I have a person in custody who's afraid to talk to me, but I think he had nothing to do with the murder. I just think he knows something that can help me put things together."

"I can't work like this. I can't just take your word for things. What if he reveals something during interrogation that makes him a suspect?"

"Talk to him yourself. Get his side. Tell me what's safe. In fact, get his story and tell me what he said hypothetically. Unless it's really bad, he'll walk away a free man. Just get him to talk so I can wrap this up."

"What assurances do I—"

"Counselor, I want the guy who put the knife in her and the guy who told him to do it. If he's not one of those guys, I think he can sleep in his own bed tonight."

Maria thought about it for a moment, biting the flesh about her thumb. When she had made up her mind, she undid her robe, showing a very short teddy and started to walk away.

"Let me get dressed."

"Thank you, Maria," Gonzalo said looking up to the ceiling to avoid seeing what his wife would not want him looking at.

"Yeah, thank you," she said, going into her bedroom. "I wanted to get into my own bed," she said closing the door on the sheriff.

A few minutes later, Maria Garcia and Gonzalo were crossing the plaza to the church.

"Do you have a list of questions you'd like me to ask him?" Maria said as they went up the steps to the church doors.

"Just ask him to tell you what he knows about Elena's murder," Gonzalo said, opening the door for Maria. "I think I have the guys responsible. Ask him if he knows the Tejada brothers. Just say it like that: 'Do you know the Tejada brothers?' "

"That's it?"

"Yeah. If he knows anything pertinent, I'll want him to testify."

Father Moreno was sitting at one of the pews at the front of the church. He stood up to greet them.

"I should undertake a study of how hard the benches are in this church."

"You're thinking of getting padded benches?" Gonzalo asked.

"No, no. I go easy enough with the penance. But

you're not here to talk about penance and pews; come with me."

Father Moreno ushered the two to the office and introduced them to Jose Salgado. Jose looked at the new people with some alarm in his face.

"I think you know the sheriff. This is Maria Garcia. She's a very good lawyer from here in town, and she is here to advise you about what you should and should not say."

The priest stepped out of the room, and Maria Garcia raised an eyebrow at the sheriff. Gonzalo took the hint and went to the pews with Father Moreno.

Maria Garcia closed the office door and pulled a chair close to her client.

"I want you to understand two things, Jose, before I ask you any questions and before you give me any information. First of all, six weeks from now, if I'm lucky, the city of Angustias will give me a check for helping you. I want to earn that check, Jose, so get that straight, I am here to help you—Angustias pays me, but I work for you, understand?"

Jose nodded.

"Good. The second thing you need to know is that you really need help at this point. There was a murder committed in this town; someone is going to go to jail for that; whoever goes to jail for that will come out of jail twenty years from now if they are lucky. So you see, we want to make sure that you are not the person who goes to jail, understand?"

Jose nodded again.

"Don't you have vocal cords? Speak."

"I understand everything."

"Good. Now, what do you know about the murder of Elena Maldonado?"

"I loved her."

Maria let the words hang in the air a moment.

"I know that, Jose. Elena spoke of you. She wanted a life with you. I know all that. But you need to put that to one side in your mind right now and tell me what you know about what happened today."

"I didn't kill her."

"I don't think you did, Jose. Even the sheriff doesn't think you did, but you know who did it, don't you? You know why they did it."

Jose nodded.

"It was Pedro Tejada. He's from Santurce."

"Why? How did he know Elena?"

"He didn't know her. . . . She didn't know people like that . . . He's bad. He's been bad since he was a kid. . . ."

"Fine. I believe you. He was bad, but how did he know Elena? Why did he kill her? Not for fun, right?"

"For money. He's killed other people for money. He killed a man in a bar in Santurce . . ."

"Jose. Concentrate on Elena. Who gave Pedro money? Do you know?"

"It was her husband. Marcos. I know that much."

"Marcos found him and hired him to kill Elena? Why?"

Tears came to the young man's eyes.

"I think he knew about me."

Maria looked up to the ceiling to try to figure out whether the story made enough sense to her. Jealousy was a recognized motive for murder. She was willing to believe that Pedro Tejada was a bad man, a killer. She tried to think if there was any difficulty in divulging her client's information to Gonzalo. The strain of trying to remember whether there were any relevant legal principles that she was forgetting began to give her a headache, and it reminded her of why she went into real estate.

"I'll be right back," she said as she left the room.

"What have you got?" Gonzalo asked, rising from his pew.

"Here's the story—Pedro Tejada was paid by Marcos Maldonado to kill Elena. Marcos found out she was having an affair—"

"That doesn't make any sense . . ."

"It doesn't?"

"Well, I mean it makes some sense in a basic way— Marcos was jealous, I could see that as a motive. But how did Marcos pick this guy? More importantly, Marcos is a hothead; there's plenty of evidence of that. Hotheads don't hire hitmen, they do it themselves. Ask him how Perfecto was involved."

"Perfecto was involved?"

"Ask Jose. Look, I'm headed over to the precinct. I'll be back in fifteen minutes or so. Get your client talking; have him come up with something that has fewer holes in it. I like him. I don't want to see him hurt."

"Are you threatening—"

"Ms. Garcia, I'm not threatening anything. He's a part of a murder investigation. I think he's a witness, not a participant. He has to be a little more forthcoming if he wants to maintain his status. Not a threat at all, just a fact. When I transport prisoners to San Juan tomorrow, I can either take the two guys in the station house alone, or I can take him along. That depends on what he gives me."

"And whether you believe him."

"And whether I believe him."

Maria Garcia headed back to the church office, leaving Gonzalo to make his way back to the station house.

Officer Estrada was in the precinct when Gonzalo walked in. He was stooped over the desk with all the papers found in La Cola and in Perfecto's shack. Officer Calderon was seated at the desk, looking at one of the papers intently through a magnifying glass.

"Anything interesting?"

"Very," Estrada said.

"Show me what you have."

Estrada picked two of the papers from the La Cola bundle and one slip of paper from Perfecto's house and headed outside with Gonzalo following.

"This paper from La Cola and this one from Perfecto's house have the same phone number in the same handwriting. The handwriting is not the same as with the other pieces that came from Perfecto's house. I'm assuming the other pieces are in Perfecto's hand, this one is not. The prefix for the phone number is in Santurce, and I'm willing to bet I know who it belongs to."

"Salgado's father?"

Estrada nodded.

"He's the connection between a decent kid like Salgado and these lowlifes."

Gonzalo looked to the ground and shook his head.

"That doesn't make perfect sense, but then maybe this murder won't be squared away perfectly."

"Well, we've only given it one afternoon. Besides, we have more . . . The rest of the papers from La Cola are like this one." He handed Gonzalo a letter, and the sheriff read several lines of it.

"This is disgusting," he said.

"This is the cleanest one. I think they're supposed to be love letters. . . ."

"But this is pornography. . . ."

"Well, like a teenager would write, I guess. But the interesting thing is that these boys were trying to plant these letters in the Maldonado house. See who they're from?"

"So you think Jose Salgado was in on this?"

"Well, I can't be sure. I think if you get writing samples from each of the three guys we have, you'll probably find they don't match Jose's handwriting."

"Pedro?"

"That would be my guess."

Gonzalo thought for a moment before reentering the precinct. Once inside, he headed to his desk and took out a yellow legal pad. He brought Pedro out of his cell, sat him at Hector's desk and passed the pad to him with a pen. Pedro took it in his still-manacled hands.

"I'm not going to tell you anything," he said.

"I know. Tomorrow, I'm taking you to San Juan. There you'll get a lawyer. But I have to do my job, so I need you to write that you are not going to tell me anything. It should say something like 'I invoke my right to remain silent about the charges brought against me in the city of Angustias on this date, etc.'"

Pedro looked at the sheriff skeptically.

"What about my handcuffs? I can't write anything with them on."

"Are you going to try to escape again?" Gonzalo asked.

"How am I going to escape? There's three of you in here."

"Okay." Gonzalo unshackled one of Pedro's wrists.

Pedro stopped as he was about to begin writing and smiled at the sheriff.

"You think I'm stupid or something?"

"What makes you say that?"

"You didn't say what the charges are against me. How can I say I refuse to talk about the charges? What are the charges?"

"What difference does it make? Do you want to talk to me about anything?"

"Ah, but then I have to say all the charges, not just the charges. I'm not stupid." Pedro put his head down and began writing. He dated his refusal to talk, and he signed it.

"There. Now don't ask me anymore questions until I get a lawyer because I'm not talking to no damn *gandule*."

"That's fine," Gonzalo said putting the handcuff back on his prisoner. "Officer Calderon, if you can please show Mr. Tejada back to his cell . . . and bring out his younger brother."

"He's not going to tell you nothing either," Pedro said as Officer Calderon was locking him into his cell.

"Oh, I don't want him to tell me anything. I want him to write his answer just like you did."

Carlos Tejada sat next to the sheriff and offered his wrists so Gonzalo could free him to write.

"Okay, here. I want you to write how you know Jose Salgado . . ."

"*No escribas na'.*" Pedro ordered. "Don't write anything."

"Look. It's a simple question. Jose is a suspect in this mess. All I want to know is where you first met him. Was it in the bar in Santurce? Was it in school? I'm not asking you to say who did what today. I understand you're not going to write about that. You're going to stick with your brother. I understand. That's fine with me. Jose's talking to us. He's cooperating. Marcos Maldonado is cooperating. Jaime Salgado has already said his side of the whole story, so you see I don't want your testimony. Everyone's pointing at you. I just think I might be able to get Jose in this too. Here, just write out like your brother did that you don't want to talk to me, etc. Copy what he wrote."

Gonzalo pushed Pedro's short statement toward Carlos. The young man hesitated for a minute or more, but finally he decided to fill out his statement using the same wording as his brother.

When Carlos was safely back in his cell, Gonzalo handed their written statements to Iris Calderon.

"Does their handwriting match any of the notes we found?"

"You can't do that!" Pedro protested, but no one paid him any attention.

"Not at all," her answer came back a minute later. "These guys are both left-handed and the writing is not. Sorry."

"Oh, don't worry. Since it's not these two, I know who wrote the letters. I just wanted to exclude them. Look. You and Estrada are going on a little road trip." He wrote out instructions onto a piece of the yellow legal-pad paper and handed it to her. She looked at it.

"Dead or alive?"

"Alive. I need him alive."

Hector walked into the precinct at this point.

"Did I miss anything?"

"Not much," Calderon said as she and Officer Estrada went out the door.

"Did you finish getting prints from the car?"

"No. I left that job half done. The car's secure at Domingo's shop."

"Here. Entertain yourself with dusting these letters. I think it should be interesting."

"Where are you headed?"

"This case is giving me a headache. I'm going to finish it."

"You know who did it?"

Gonzalo looked up and thought a moment before answering.

"Let's just say the list of suspects is getting real short, real fast."

CHAPTER TWENTY

It was a little past eight o'clock in the evening when Estrada and Calderon headed out on the road to Santurce. Calderon drove and faced almost no traffic in entering the metropolitan area. They had only to wait fifteen or twenty minutes to get through *El Tapon de Bayamon* that had slowed Estrada by an hour earlier in the day.

Once in Santurce, the two officers went first to the precinct there to declare their intentions. The desk sergeant on duty at that moment rolled his eyes as they approached, and the officers were glad to think that he would not be one to ask too many questions and certainly would not be willing to demand to take part in the action they intended.

"What are you guys doing here?"

"We're here to bring in one Jaime Salgado for questioning."

"Where do you plan to take him?"

"We're here from Angustias," Calderon spoke.

"Angustias? Where the Hell is that?"

Estrada tried to explain how to get there from Santurce, but the sergeant wasn't interested.

"Okay, okay. Look. I assume this questioning has something to do with prostitution?"

"We really don't know," Calderon said. "If you want, you can talk to our sheriff. I think he can clear up any questions."

The sergeant put up his hand to keep her from going on.

"Do you two need backup? No? Good. Do what you have to do, but don't make a mess in my city, okay guys?"

The officers left the precinct, and Estrada gave Calderon directions to the bar where he had seen Jaime Salgado late that afternoon.

"Who do you want to go in first?" Calderon asked as they were about to enter the bar.

"What do you mean? We can go in together."

"But if he sees you, he might know what it's all about, don't you think?"

"He's going to know sooner or later, isn't he?"

"Yeah, but I think if I go in, I'll catch him off-guard . . ."

"Okay, if you want. I'll wait out here."

Estrada gave her a description of Jaime Salgado: "five-foot-five, thin, a scraggly beard on a wrinkled face, a Gilligan's hat on his head"—told her which booth he had been at then crossed his arms and stood facing the door. Calderon went into the bar after undoing the snap that guarded the mace canister on her gun belt.

Jaime Salgado was sitting with one of the prostitutes in his employ at the same booth Estrada had seen him in earlier. He was joking with the woman and pinching her midsection. The woman seemed to want no part of him but was afraid to move away from the man who called her his.

"Jaime Salgado?" Calderon asked.

He looked up and shook his head.

"I never heard of Jaime Salgado," he said, and he gave his prostitute another pinch, harder this time so that she involuntarily inched away from him. He grabbed her by the elbow and she knew enough to move closer again.

"Well, do you know where I can find Jaime Salgado? I hear he is a very ugly man with no testicles." Calderon hoped to provoke a more useful answer from Jaime, but really pimps made her sick and in the back of her mind, she wanted this little man to resist her so she could hurt him.

"I told you, I don't know any Jaime Salgado. But if you're interested in testicles, I can show you a—"

"Why don't you just show me your ID? A driver's license would be good. Then we can clear up my mistake in a second."

Jaime shrugged, stood up slowly, and reached into his pocket. He kept his eyes on Calderon's face while he went through this motion, then eyed the front door quickly. Calderon knew instantly that he was planning to bolt, but in that instant he shoved her in the chest sending her back onto some bar stools. He ran for the door while Calderon straightened herself and began to chase.

"Estrada!" she yelled as Jaime hit the barroom door.

Officer Estrada stepped into the doorway as Jaime was coming out and as he put out his arm to arrest the suspect, the suspect put out his elbow to catch the officer in the face. Jaime hit hard, and Estrada lost his balance falling backwards as Jaime had hoped, but he already had his hands on Jaime's shirt and arm when he fell. While Estrada landed on his back, Jaime hit the sidewalk with his face. A second later, Calderon came out of the bar to find Estrada sitting up on the sidewalk with one hand at his newly bruised eye and the other keeping Jaime Salgado's face on the pavement.

"Sorry about that," Calderon told her partner as she cuffed the prisoner after reading him his rights.

"At least my eyes match now. That was beginning to worry me," he answered.

"Are you guys going to take me to the precinct here?" Jaime asked. "I'm filling out a report on police brutality . . ."

"You assaulted me, you idiot," Estrada told him as he was being put in the cruiser.

"That's for a judge to decide."

"Look. You're being arrested for the murder of Elena Maldonado over in Angustias—"

"I've never even been to Angustias!"

"That's not what we hear. Everyone says it was you. Your son says it was you, Marcos says it . . ."

Calderon tried to interrupt Estrada with a stare, but he went on.

"Those two Tejada brothers swear you were there this afternoon. They've got the sheriff pretty convinced there's only one way to go in this investigation."

"It wasn't me—"

"Stop it!" Estrada yelled at him.

"We have your fingerprints there; lying isn't going to help you. You have the right to remain silent; use it."

The trio was halfway to Angustias before Jaime Salgado spoke again.

"What did Marcos say? Because you have to understand . . . Marcos is a liar; everybody knows it."

"Oh yeah?" Calderon answered, taking a look at him in the backseat through the rearview mirror. "What about the Tejada guys?"

"They're even worse . . . They'll say anything . . . You have to watch out for the older one. He'll do anything . . ."

"What about your son?"

Jaime was quiet for a moment.

"He's never been arrested. He might say anything . . . You know, because he's afraid. But believe me . . . if someone was killed, he doesn't have any facts about it. In fact, you guys can let him go. I swear to you, he doesn't know about this crime. . . ."

"What crime does he know about?" Calderon asked.

"Nothing. He don't know anything. He's innocent . . . I swear."

"Don't swear. Tell us what you know."

Jaime threw himself back in his seat.

"It was Perfecto. Him and his stupid religion. He started everything."

"Very convenient. Blame the dead guy for it. Am I supposed to believe Perfecto stabbed his own daughter? Come on . . . He was bad, but he wasn't that bad, was he?"

"No, no. He didn't stab her, but he got her killed, anyway."

"Do you want to explain that a little?"

"Can you make a deal with me? You got that kind of authority?"

"You want to wait to talk to the sheriff?"

"Sure. I'll talk to him. What's his name?"

"Gonzalo."

"Gonzalo? Where have I heard that name before? Did he do anything? Maybe a long time ago?"

"He solved the Nestor Ochoa case a couple of years ago."

"Ah, now I remember. Didn't he have a case in Angustias . . . I don't even know how many years ago . . . A little girl got raped, something like that?

You wouldn't remember, that's how long ago I'm talking about . . . I know about that case."

"What do you know?" Calderon was staring at him through the rearview mirror so intently that both Estrada in the passenger seat and Jaime in the back were a bit worried.

"I know what I've heard. . . . Pay attention to the road; you're drifting."

"What have you heard?"

"You're drifting," he said louder, but she wouldn't take her eyes off him.

"Look, I'll deal with the sheriff," Jaime said with real fear in his voice. They could all hear gravel kicking up under the car, which meant they were going off the road and might soon be headed into a tree or off the hill altogether or—even worse—they might be driving into the cement walls of one of the houses lining the road. She gave her passenger one last glare before slowing the car and bringing it back onto the road.

"Jesus, lady. I said I'd talk to the sheriff."

"Make sure that you tell him everything. Remember, I'm transporting you to San Juan nice and early in the morning."

The rest of the trip to Angustias was taken in silence. Jaime refused to look anywhere but out the window, afraid that he might further distract the deputy. Estrada cast occasional side glances at his partner, and Calderon kept her eyes on the road the rest of the way with only a slight smile to show what she was thinking of.

In Angustias, Gonzalo had already spoken with Marcos when his deputies returned. He was sitting in his car in front of the precinct. Estrada got out and approached him before getting Jaime out of the squad car.

"How's it going?" Estrada asked.

"Oh, everything's fine here. We have the guilty parties." Gonzalo smiled as he said this.

"More than one?"

"Yeah. Remind me . . . next budget increase, we need another station house. I've got no place to put Mr. Salgado."

"Well, I think you're going to want to talk to him. Calderon has him scared out of his mind."

"I see you got a bruise to match your other eye."

"Salgado's elbow."

"On purpose?"

"Yeah, resisting."

"Go home. You look terrible."

"I want to see the end of this case," Estrada pleaded.

"You can barely see anything. Look, you've seen the end of it."

"What? Everyone's going to jail?"

"Except Jose Salgado. He's the only clean one in all of this. Mostly clean. Clean enough to go home."

"So how does it all work out? Who did what? Why did they kill her? For what?"

"You want to know? You and Calderon can follow me with Salgado. You'll see everything you want." Gonzalo put his car in gear and pulled out. Calderon followed close behind in the squad car.

"Where are we going?" Jaime asked after a minute or two of driving, but he was ignored since neither deputy knew where they were going, and a few minutes later the question was answered.

Gonzalo pulled into a driveway that was only indifferently hacked into the tall grass and which had once been graveled. There were patches of gravel now, but most of it had been washed away with the rain of months and years. It was the driveway of Perfecto Cruz and the only way to reach his house without a machete. The two cars went over a low rise and Perfecto's shack loomed ugly in front of them. Gonzalo got out of his car, leaving the headlights on and pulled out both the flashlight from his gun belt and the larger flashlight he had used earlier. He entered the shack and waved on his deputies.

"Bring the prisoner!" he shouted to them, and they did.

"Here," he said putting the only chair in the center of the room. "Have a seat, Mr. Salgado."

Salgado sat and took a look around the room, finding, of course, not much to look at.

"What is this place? It looks deserted . . . What are you guys going to do to me?" Gonzalo could tell Salgado was afraid he might never leave the room alive.

"We're not going to do anything to you. You're not worth it . . ."

"I've got information. Ask the woman."

Calderon went to Gonzalo's side and whispered in his ear.

"He's says he knows about this case and the little girl from twenty-five years ago."

Gonzalo jerked his head back slightly from the mention of this case. He looked down, trying to re-arrange how he was going to approach the questioning of his prisoner. He had planned on being direct. In fact, he had planned on little more than confronting Jaime with the story Marcos Maldonado had given him and letting the two liars bring him to some center of truth. After all, he had enough physical evidence to charge all of them with conspiracy to murder Elena Maldonado. Jaime was more important to him now. There were only a few cases he had not solved to his satisfaction in the twenty-six years he had been sheriff of Angustias. His first murder case had been of a three-year-old girl who went missing for more than a day. The entire town had gone into the woods and fields looking for her, but it was Gonzalo who found her toddling out of a clump of tall grass, crying without tears, her clothes torn, blood flowing from her vagina. He rushed her to the clinic where nothing could be done for her. She died in his arms, and every day since then at least once before he drifted off to sleep, she died in his eyes again. There was little he wanted more in the world than to catch the man who had killed the girl and make him pay.

He paced the room.

"Tell me about the girl," he said calmly.

Salgado smiled.

"First, tell what deal you have for me."

Gonzalo stood in front of Salgado in his chair. He lunged, knocking over Salgado and chair, landing on top of the prisoner on the floor, choking him with both hands on his throat. After Salgado was convinced he was going to die in that one-room shack, Gonzalo lifted him by the throat and slammed him into the floor several times.

"You want a deal?" Gonzalo whispered through clenched teeth. "Tell me about the girl, and I won't kill you. There's your deal."

Salgado nodded his agreement to the deal offered him, and Gonzalo let him go. Salgado gagged for more than a minute and the sheriff began to lose patience.

"I'm not hearing anything about the girl," he said, and Salgado pled with his eyes.

"Give me a second," he coughed out.

"No. This is going to get painful . . ." He reached for his nightstick.

"It was an American. . . . I'm sure of it. . . . I know. I don't know his name. White. Very white.

Young in those days, maybe thirty. No more than thirty. Blond. Mustache . . ."

"How do you know this?"

"I . . . dealt with him."

"What do you mean?"

"He came to me . . . Before he did anything to the girl, he came to me . . . He said he wanted a girl . . . you know, a young girl . . ."

"And what did you do?"

"Please . . . I was a bad man then . . ."

"You're a *pimp*." Gonzalo put all the disgust he was capable of in the last word.

"I was worse, believe me. I'm better now . . ."

"What did you do?"

"I got him the youngest I had . . . I got him a twelve-year-old. Her mother owed me—"

Gonzalo slapped him out of his chair with the back of his hand.

"I'm not going to say anymore if you keep hitting me!"

Gonzalo pulled out his revolver and both his deputies turned away not knowing where to look.

"Then I don't need you anymore," Gonzalo said as he aimed at the prisoner.

"I'll talk!" Salgado screamed. "Please! I'll talk! He didn't want the girl. Too old . . . that's what he said. Then he left. The next day, the girl was missing. The day after, she was dead. I'm positive it was him."

"Did you see him again?"

"Nope. Never again."

"Where was he from?"

"I really don't know . . . Honest, I really don't know. He had an accent . . ."

"Of course he had an accent; he was an *Americano*, you said . . ."

"I mean a strange one for an *Americano;* he wasn't from New York . . ."

"From the south?"

"I don't think so . . . Look, I don't know anything about *gringo* accents. He just sounded funny. I swear, this is all I know."

Gonzalo paced the room, and Salgado slowly rose to his feet.

"Are you going to put the gun away?" the prisoner asked.

Gonzalo looked down at his gun hand.

"No. Come with me."

Gonzalo gave Salgado a shove out the door of the shack, and used a flashlight to illuminate the path he wanted the prisoner to walk. They went around the house to Perfecto's toolshed.

Inside the boxes and appliances had been dusted for fingerprints, the black dust was on a dozen items and Hector Pareda was peeling tape off an item by the light of a flashlight.

"Recognize any of this stuff?"

"I never saw—"

"Let's not start this, Salgado. Just one of your fingerprints is enough to make you a liar. That won't help you."

"Okay. I had a deal with Perfecto. He was supposed to get me this stuff. I didn't tell him to steal any of it. . . . How he got it is his business. . . ."

"How did he get it, Hector?" Gonzalo asked.

Hector pulled out a small notepad from his shirt pocket.

"Most of this is missing from a warehouse in Santurce. The guard was beaten senseless by a man roughly fitting Perfecto's description. . . . A van was backed up and driven off."

"So that's his crime, not mine," Salgado said.

"Yeah. Somebody might think that. But Perfecto had the address of this warehouse in his pocket. It wasn't in his handwriting. You didn't happen to write it out for him, did you? Well, I don't even have to ask you. . . . There are fingerprints on that piece of paper too."

"Goddamn that Perfecto," Salgado said after a few seconds of thought. "There are rocks with more brains than him."

"Yeah, well it gets more interesting. You want to hear what Marcos Maldonado had to say about these appliances?"

Salgado shook his head.

"Who's more stupid, Salgado? The idiot or the man who does business with the idiot?"

"I want a lawyer."

"Oh, you'll get one. He'll be the only person to visit you while you spend twenty-five years in jail."

Estrada hustled Salgado back to the squad car.

Calderon and Gonzalo followed, leaving Hector to his work.

"You weren't really going to shoot him, right?"

Gonzalo shrugged.

"You weren't just going to stand there if you thought I was going to kill him, right?"

They made the rest of the trip back to their cars in silence.

CHAPTER TWENTY-ONE

Back at the center of town, Gonzalo parked once again in front of the station house, hoping he would hear nothing to cause him to run out again. He got out of his car slowly. His shift wasn't supposed to end for a while yet, but he felt drained. A normal day as sheriff of Angustias wasn't nearly as stressful as this one had been. Usually there were only a few turns to take about the town to make everyone aware that he was on duty and possibly a drunk or two to handle at Colmado Ruiz. Though the number of officers at his command this day was more than it had been just a few years earlier, though the station house had been expanded recently as well, he knew that it could be said of him that he should have called upon the larger resources of *Los Metropolitanos*.

"To Hell with it," he said to himself as he got out of the car. "We caught them."

He walked over to Calderon and Estrada as they were taking Jaime out of their car.

"Keep him here for a while until I think of a place for him to spend the night. I'll be back in a few minutes."

He walked over to the church and strode down the center aisle toward the offices in the back. Father Moreno accosted him as he walked.

"Sheriff Gonzalo . . . Please . . . I cannot allow you to keep a suspect here overnight."

"Father . . . Please . . ."

"I can't have it, Sheriff. This church cannot be a warehouse for criminals, suspected criminals, deputies and their guns. You understand my position, don't you?"

"I understand, but I think you're wrong. . . . Angustias needs the help of the church, and the church doesn't want to give it. There are some that might see this the wrong way. . . ."

"But Maria Garcia tells me you could take this prisoner to San Juan. . . . He could get a lawyer there, and they have the facilities to handle him properly. . . ."

"Father, have you ever been to the prison in San Juan? If you want to talk about how prisoners should be handled. . . . In San Juan, he would be one of dozens processed tonight. He'd be squeezed into a single cell with twenty other guys—drunks, drug addicts, male prostitutes, murderers, rapists. . . . they all go in together. A young man like that—small, afraid, no friends—he'll probably be beaten or raped or both before sunrise. But don't worry, Father . . . I understand."

Gonzalo kept walking toward the office. Father Moreno followed close behind.

"I don't think he had anything to do with Elena's murder, Sheriff."

"I know he didn't, Father."

Gonzalo knocked on the door to the office and Maria Garcia opened and stepped out into the hallway with the sheriff.

"Tell your client he is a material witness in the case of the murder of Elena Maldonado. Most importantly, he is to remain on the island and continue residing at his address in Naranjito. He is not to have contact with the principles of the case. I'll provide you with a list. Also, his car is impounded as evidence in this same case."

"How will he get home?"

"You can drive him or one of my deputies can drive him. You choose."

Gonzalo opened the office door.

"Take his cuffs off, Anibal. He's a free man."

"Aye, aye, captain."

Gonzalo rolled his eyes at the title, but it was a motion the deputy did not see and would not have understood.

"Which is it, Counselor? Do you want to take him or should I send Anibal?"

"I'll take him. One thing . . . Is the case solved? Are all the loose ends tied up?"

"The short answer is yes. I'll get you a report after the prisoners are transported tomorrow. It will give you the outline of the case and where your client fits in. You'll be better able to advise him once you have it, so you might want to schedule a meeting with him for tomorrow afternoon. That is, if you intend to advise him further."

"When do I have to let you know?"

"He's not a suspect . . . you don't have to let me know anything. You can just advise him of his rights and responsibilities as a witness and send Angustias a bill for your services. Send one for Carmen Ortiz too."

Maria Garcia left with her client.

"What do you want me to do?" Anibal asked.

"Go to the clinic. Tell Marcos Maldonado that he is officially charged with the murder of Elena Maldonado."

"He is?"

"Yes. When you tell him, read him his rights."

"We already read him his rights."

"It won't hurt to do it again. Read him his rights and stay with him. Make sure he speaks to no one about this case. Only doctors and nurses, okay?"

"Sure. How long do you want me to sit with him?"

"Take a book."

Father Moreno stopped Gonzalo before he left the church.

"I thought you were going to leave a prisoner here. . . ."

"Not if it can be avoided, Father."

"Then what was that whole story for?"

"It was for you, Father. You are part of a community. The church shouldn't separate itself. Believe me . . . I don't put prisoners in a church just for the fun of it."

As Gonzalo was crossing the plaza to the *alcaldía*, Don Julio peered out the door of his house.

"*¿Terminamos?*" "Are we done?"

Gonzalo stopped in the middle of the plaza, feeling Don Julio was owed something of an explanation of the day's events because of his service to Angustias.

"Yes. We . . ."

Don Julio closed his door before anymore could be said.

In the *alcaldía*, Gonzalo entered the deputy mayor's office. Officer Vargas was staring at some of the books on the shelves, his hands behind his back. Marrero was asleep and snoring, his chin resting on his chest.

Vargas turned to face his sheriff.

"Are you relieving me?" Vargas laughed.

"Almost." Gonzalo went over to the prisoner and gave him a nudge to wake him.

"What? What? What?" Marrero woke up as though terrified.

"Wake up, Marrero."

"Can I get a drink? I know Nuñez keeps liquor in here someplace. . . . Check his desk drawers. He has to have some. . . ."

"Shut up, Marrero. Go home."

"I'm not under arrest anymore?"

"You're under house arrest. Go home. We'll pick you up in the morning."

"How early?"

"How does nine sound to you?"

"Too early, man. I can't do that—"

"If you can't do that, I have to keep you here. Do you want that?"

"Does Nuñez have something to drink or not?"

"Nothing."

"Then let me go. Just knock really hard tomorrow."

Gonzalo undid Marrero's handcuffs.

"I bet you didn't figure out this murder."

"I've got a good idea. . . ."

"Tell me."

"Perfecto hired the Tejada brothers to kill Marcos, right?"

Marrero looked genuinely surprised.

"How'd you figure that out?"

"That's what Marcos told me. I assume that's what he told you too."

"So you're going to let him go too?"

"What? You think I'm stupid enough to believe him?"

"I believed him."

"Yeah, I know."

"So what happened?"

"You'll find out later. For now, just remember to be home tomorrow at nine."

Gonzalo and Officer Vargas walked Marrero to the door of the *alcaldia*.

"So what did happen?" Vargas asked once Marrero was out of earshot.

"Like I said. Perfecto hired Pedro Tejada to kill Marcos."

"Then what?"

"Wait until we get to the station."

Gonzalo and Vargas made their way around to where Calderon and Estrada were waiting with their prisoner.

"Jaime Salgado, stand up," Gonzalo ordered.

Jaime rose from his seat in the patrol car.

"Your son has been set free. His testimony will help put you in jail. Do you understand that?"

"He won't testify against his own father."

"He already did. I just need you to confirm one detail. If you can't confirm it, I think your son might be joining you in jail. You understand?"

Jaime looked confused, so Gonzalo repeated his question, and Jaime nodded.

"Good. Your son was a friend of Carlos Tejada, right?"

Jaime looked at each of the officers in turn. His face plainly said he had no idea where this was going.

"Okay, let me make it easier for you. When I look up school records tomorrow, I'm going to find that Carlos and Jose went to the same school, they sat in the same class, maybe even right next to each other in alphabetical order, right?"

"I don't know what you're going to find. I don't know where they sat."

"Right. Okay. Get in the car."

Jaime Salgado sat and Gonzalo closed the car door after him. The officers moved to some distance from the car before Gonzalo explained the case to them in low tones.

"Perfecto contacted Jaime not just to find a suitable boyfriend for his daughter. Sooner or later, he wanted a hitman to kill Marcos, maybe once he found out about the money. Maybe Marcos did something to piss him off, personally. There was a problem. Perfecto hired the brothers through Jaime Salgado. Elena knew Marcos had inherited land worth millions. Since Elena knew, Jose Salgado knew. Since Jose knew, his father knew. Since his father knew, the killers knew.

"Jaime, Pedro, and Carlos cooked up a scheme. They told Marcos about the plan against him. He hired them to kill Elena instead and plant the love letters to make it look like Jose did it."

"But Jaime loves his son," Calderon interjected.

"Why? Because he thinks his son is good? Because he thinks his son loves him? Jaime Salgado is about as low as a human can go. He would sell out his son in a second for a million dollars. Don't underestimate a bad man's ability to do evil. Anyway, this is easy to solve. Check his handwriting against the letters. I'll bet you three days vacation, Jaime wrote the notes."

"But if they were working for Perfecto . . ." Estrada began.

"Perfecto stole a truckload of goods as payment. Street value five thousand dollars. Ten thousand to be generous. Once Jaime knew there could be millions from Marcos, Perfecto was stuck with the goods. They took Jose's car to make sure it looked like Elena's lover did it. They hid out in La Cola trying to figure out Jose's routine with Elena."

"What about Perfecto's prints on the weapon?" Estrada asked.

"I don't doubt they used Perfecto's knife to kill his own daughter. Maybe he even gave it to them when he thought they were going to kill Marcos. No difference. They killed her. Pedro stabbed; Carlos drove. If they had planted the letters when they killed her, we might never have known."

"You're confident about all this? It looks like a hard case to make," Calderon asked.

"I arrest people, collect evidence and charge them. The prosecutor makes the case. I'm confident of one thing—there's enough guilt for all of them to share. By the time they finish accusing each other and making deals, they'll all be sitting in jail."

EPILOGUE

Hours later, after he had typed out his own four-page, single spaced report and supervised the writing of similar reports from his deputies and checked everything for spelling and grammar mistakes, Gonzalo went home. It was only after he had quietly closed the door behind himself that he remembered that he was supposed to have brought home the infant's clothes. He calmed himself with the thought that the child couldn't possibly be in that great a need of clothes—a blanket would do to cover his nakedness until morning when his clothes could be fetched.

He took off his shoes and tiptoed to his daughter's room. She was sound asleep, not having been bothered all day with anything more vexing than playing with her grandmother's chickens, climbing trees, and chasing grasshoppers. He envied her peace.

He showered and tried to think of any stones he may have left unturned. Lost deep in thoughts that soon made no sense, he nodded off with the cool water gently beating on his face. When a deep breath sucked water up his nose, he woke up and finished his bath.

"Did I wash my hair?" he wondered as he dried himself off, then he decided he didn't really care.

He wrapped a towel around himself, went to the kitchen, opened the refrigerator and found nothing he wanted to eat.

In the bedroom, Mari was awake and looking at him and there was no baby. His wife put an arm up out towards him. He knew there was nothing he could say to heal her. In a few short hours the child had gained her affections, and Gonzalo knew better than anyone in the world that Mari's feelings always had an irresistible power, and they were long-lived. He had based his own life on the strength of her heart.

Gonzalo went to his wife and held her.

"They took him," she said.

"I know," Gonzalo answered, but there was nothing more for him to say.

The agency in charge of placing the Maldonado child found relatives on Elena's side of the family living in Florida. They were good people; Mari made sure to find that out. The boy, named Gilberto by his new family, spent the first four years of his life like any other child in Florida.

In the fifth year of his life, his father, Marcos Maldonado, still in prison for the murder of his mother, died. While his coconspirators had been forced to serve the time given them without the money for appeals, he had sold away ten acres paying for his. Told by his lawyer that he was within days of finally winning his freedom, he had alcohol smuggled in to him at his cell. He got drunk, angered most of the other inmates in his cellblock and was found in his cell, hanged with his own bedsheets. There was a halfhearted investigation that declared he had hung himself. There was evidence to the contrary—plainly heard screams, bruises on his face and fists—but no one could be found to care enough about his end to reopen the investigation.

The thirty-nine acres he had not yet liquidated were passed on to Gilberto. Maria Garcia, having never lost sight of the boy she considered her client, sent a note to the family asking if they wanted her to sell the land and send on the proceeds. They, having no idea what the land was worth, asked that she set up a trust fund for the child. The government did expand the Number Two Highway and Gilberto became a millionaire.

In the years since that night, Mari has visited the child twice. The first time was when he was still an infant. She had pictures of herself taken with him in her arms, pictures she treasures still. The second time was when he was six. Maria Garcia went with her to deliver a reckoning to the adoptive parents and to give them money from the trust fund for his expenses and private school.

Mari stayed with the family for a week, taking Gilberto to school and to church on Sunday. She saw him at play with his adoptive brother and sister. She saw him at play with his schoolmates. She saw him at play with neighborhood children. She saw him laughing every day she was there, and she was finally able to let him go. Since then, she has sent him birthday cards and Christmas presents, and he has sent her thank-you notes, and they have both been happy.